First Edition May 2017

Author's Preface

If you have followed my previous work you will have met Rose at her final moments; known as Nanna Rose; then an appearance 16 years before that when she appeared at the pyre of Ma'Beths body.

Well I can promise you I will answer some of those questions you are wondering; however I say this to you.

"He who says there are only two sides to a story; have never held a rubix cube…"

And End: And a Beginning

Rose Marie Munro; born in Bayswater, London.

"Sir please, we need you out of the way..." The midwife shouted.

Richard knelt by the ornate four poster bed, his hands grasping his wife's limp fingers. His eyes were red and puffed.

"Do not go my love. There is still so much that we have to do together... and our daughter..." His voice faded into silence.

The aged doctor fumbled with his stethoscope and his pocket watch, nudging Richard so that the hand he so dearly held fell away like the dying petal of a rose.

Blood soaked; the Egyptian white sheets turned crimson; as the life blood ebbed from Heather.

Finally, the doctor removed the stethoscope and dropped his head as though in prayer.

*

The funeral was held at Kensal Green Cemetery. Very few people attended; as Richard's family had all passed before him. As for Heather's, well she had not wanted anything to do with them and Richard wished to keep his promise to his departed wife.

The bagpipes played their eerie tune, a lament for the passing of his dear Heather.

Richard stood there until all that was left was his daughter and her nursemaid.

He walked back along the Thames, disregarding his driver.

Shouts in the streets became more prominent. Young boys scurried around with bundles of papers under their arms.

"WAR DECLARED! READ ALL ABOUT IT"

The year was 1914. Shortly after he buried his beloved wife, Richard was called to service of the King.

In the fields of Flanders Captain Munro lay. His body lay limp; surrounded by the men he lead against a German trench, in what was known as no-man's land.

By the age of six, Rose was little more than a slave to the woman bequeathed to look after her. The Nanny who had been thrice married and subsequently had poisoned each one was now using the inheritance to sustain her lavish lifestyle.

Rose; unaware of her heritage or her father's dwindling money, kept the house clean and neat. Her education had been the stolen hours between sunrise and sunset, or when her guardian left to indulge men's fancies. By the age of twelve; the ex-Nanny tried in vain to sell Rose into marriage.

Rose had learnt to read, and although she was still under the control of her guardian (and would be until the age of twenty one).

If she were to be married the Nanny could launch a legal claim to seize what was left of her father's inheritance that he had left her.

Every suitor who came she found a way to annoy or disgust. She knew the chains of marriage would bind her to an unhappier fate.
How did she know you ask?
She saw it in the leaves that were left at the bottom of her cup.
Yes our Rose was something more than just an unlucky parentless girl, being taken advantage of.

Through chance she had learnt to read signs left in the bottom of tea cups. To her surprise, the servants in the area did not shy away from her; rather they were drawn towards her.

By the time the Nanny had learnt of

Rose's gift, it was already too late. The one thing that she had learnt from her Nanny was how to use poisons to their best effect.

Arsenic in the afternoon tea each day brought her guardian and her schemes to an untimely demise.

Rose Munro was free.

*

When the lawyer came to the house on the burial of her guardian; more was to be revealed.

"Miss Rose Munro." said the fat lawyer behind the mahogany desk. His brow creased as he looked at the rolled parchment. His lips plapped as he read and re read the letters in front of him. "It appears, young lady, that you have been served a disservice... The house and its belongings never belonged to your Nanny... However, that said and done, the debts owing because of her stewardship have amounted so much that the property's capital is now owned by the bank..."

Rose's heart sank. Where would she go from here?
"Sir... Might I enquire...? I have no recollection of my mother or any family I may have?" She trembled asking for hope beyond hope that someone may take her in.
Once again he plapped his lips. It was

so annoying that she wanted nothing more than to scold him with the hot tea in the pot; that she had just made for him. Instead she poured her own and let the leaves settle.

"It is written that your mother's surname, before the marriage to your father, was Wolbear..." He stopped for a moment and stroked his enormous third chin. "I recall reading that same name in the Times this morning." he mused.
She waited in anticipation for his next sentence, she found herself leaning forward in anticipation she could feel the leather of the chair re-inflating against her backside as she did so.
"The name related to a young man who has been taken into custody for

the suspected murder... Of err... What was it now...?" his fingers went to his brow. 'If only he hadn't left the day's copy in his study before coming here.' The lawyer thought to himself.

Rose picked up her tea to hide the anticipation. It burnt her lips on touch but she held it together, to make sure she didn't spray this old codger with tea, in the hope that he would continue his thought process.

The old lawyer raised his left buttock off the seat and ripped out a large flatulent sound, reverberating from the soft leather.

"Better out than in..." he groaned.

It seemed to Rose, that his anus was connected to his brain.

"That was it... A man called McFarlane... Reports say that this 'Wolbear' character was found covered in blood hovering over the remains of McFarlane. He's been taken to the Old Bailey pending a court hearing..." Rose's heart skipped a beat. The Old Bailey were notorious on priding themselves in incarcerating anyone, even if they were innocent.

"Is there anything Sir, that is not owned by the bank..." asked Rose. She felt at a loss. Everything that should have been hers had been taken by a thief and now the only link she knew to her mother's family was about to be hung out to dry.

He cleared his throat and once more raised his cheeks from the chair... But this time it was to pull out a silvery looking chain.

"This had special instructions from your father Miss Rose. It was your mother's pendant that was to be given to you either at the age of twenty-one, or as is now the case, the only thing you have left. That, and I believe 40 shillings."

His hand leaned forward nonchalantly. The pendant dangling free of his fat tobacco stained fingers.

A depiction of St Christopher set into the oblong silver blank plate of a pendant. It glimmered in the little sunlight that bled through into the room. As Rose reached for it, he let it slip from his hand into her slender but calloused hands.

She turned it over and over in her hands, trying to make sense of her feelings.

"In these circumstances a girl such as of yourself may find work in another household, should you wish me to enquire..." his derogative tone told her the reason for the remark. It was due to her skin colour.

Although she was not black, she was neither the pure white that polite society mixed with, only expected to serve.

His eyes lingered on her breasts longer than was comfortable; making

Rose pull her tunic closer together...
"I should wish Sir sometime to
compose myself before accepting any
offers of employment". He plapped
once more and drunk his tea in one
gulp. The cup returned to its saucer,
and as she looked up, he was already
struggling to his feet.

"The bank will require acquisition of
the property by the end of the week
Miss. So I suggest you spend your last
remaining few days seeking some
employ." With this and a last glance at
her bosoms he left.
She slumped in the chair waiting for
the all too familiar sound of the heavy
outside door closing.
'SLAM'
She leant over to his cup. The leaves

remained within. She swirled it around and around and then flipped the cup on its saucer. As she lifted it from the saucer, she saw that the pattern concluded how she felt about the man. A bigot and a rapist by nature. She grabbed her cooled tea and once more performed the same ritual. Round and round and drop.

The pattern on the saucer was a perfect symbol of the Wolf. A deathly omen. But whose death did it represent?

The Trial, The Farce and The Unknown Family

For the rest of the day, Rose sauntered about the house that should have been hers. Deliberating over a copy of The Times she had managed to get from the boy up the road. Luckily his mother had come to her for a reading not so long ago that had helped. Thus, the paper was free.

The Times newspaper spread across the mahogany desk. The front page raved about wolf attacks and people in hospitals. It was page 10 that said about the case of Wolbear and McFarlen. It was a few tiny paragraphs stating that McFarlen, of no fixed abode, was found dead in an alley; and Wolbear was discovered near the body covered in blood. Wolbear had been charged with murder and the hearing at the Old Bailey was a clear cut case, because of this, it was scheduled to take place the following day.

When she packed up the newspaper she decided to spend time and go through the house to try and find any details of her mother and father. Alas to no avail.

When the morning came, she awoke in her cot that she had always slept in. Her dreams during the night were different to normal. She pictured herself in woods. It was strange as the only woods she had ever seen were in black and white photos, but the dream picture showed all different types' greens and browns that she had never dreamed of, and as she looked deeper into her dream; she saw other colours running through the earth, into the roots and through the trunks. Then into the leaves themselves. The colours looked like sparks of light intermingled with water.

She shook her long splayed brown hair and walked naked to the water jug and bowl. It had been the first time in a long while she had afforded herself the luxury of not having to get dressed. It felt natural and cleansing, for the air to touch her body.

She poured the water in and sunk her face into the bowl washing away the sleep that stuck to her.

Her hair fell in, both parting and clumping at the same time, like tendrils of tree roots. She pulled her face out and as she did so, her hair flicked water about the room. She no longer cared. This wasn't going to be her home soon.

She walked nimbly past the droplets on the stone floor like a tightrope walker, taking calculating steps so as not to fall over. She had hung her dress on a line across the pantry that doubled up as her room. The time she had spent serving to the woman that was supposed to look after her, made her stomach turn; especially as she thought of what her father had wished for her. The dress fell over her all too easily. She kicked on her shoes with vehemence, and her toe burst through the front of the shoe.

"Damn it..." She cursed; she stopped and looked around, expecting to be scorned for her blasphemous outburst. It was strange as there was none.

She kicked off her shoes and looked at them... They were so worn through that she could feel the soles ready for falling off. Today she had no inhibitions, no one to tell her what she couldn't do or say.

She went up the back stairs to the Nanny's old bedroom. The room stank from the body she had found lying dead. It was somewhat satisfying watching her die from the Arsenic she put in her tea every day. Thankfully, the Nanny had a fetish for shoes and there feet were of similar size.

She had been flogged once; just for looking at these shoes... Now they were hers... If only the old crone had lived to see her putting these on.

For a moment she stood admiring the new shoes and then the strangest sensation came over her. Like a droplet of water that falls from an icicle and lands perfectly on the neck as your scrubbing the front porch in the winter. The one that continues to course down the spine, winding between the vertebrae.
She shivered and glanced around the room. Maybe she DID see!
Rose walked from the room with her head held high.

*

Walking out into the street seemed strange; today was the first time she could remember, that she'd used the front door as opposed to the lower servant's door.
The street gawkers looked through her. She had always been told she had dirty skin, but to her it was the only link until now, to her mother.

It was a long walk to the Old Bailey; where murderers and thieves were put on trial; to be honest they all knew that if you weren't guilty, you soon would be.

The street seemed to be teeming, with a number of strange looking people.

The usual Street scene was men in suits and bowlers and women in their smart dresses; but today of all days the road was packed with men in varying attire, from slacks to bedclothes. The women seemed the most extreme; they wore trousers and blouses. As she walked past a group of these strangers a woman knocked into her.

"I am sorry..." Rose began. Then she noticed that at the gape of her throat sat a similar pendant that also now sat in hers. The woman narrowed her brow and looked her up and down as though working out how much money she was carrying. Finally after the visual undressing, she stuck her hand out.

Her voice awkward and heavily accented, "Welcome sister... Although, I not recognise you!?"
Rose was taken aback; no one had ever called her sister.

"I'm sorry... I'm afraid you must have me mistaken..."

With this the woman grabbed Rose's jaw and twisted her head firmly from side to side. Her hands calloused; dug into her cheeks. The smell of nicotine

lingered as the clamp of her fingers
rocked down to her nape. The
pendant grasped gently. Her eyes
narrowed.

"Have you stole this girl?" her voice
suddenly serious.
Rose flustered and felt her face glow.

"It's mine... My mother left it to me."

She stepped back and in doing so the
woman let the pendant drop from her
grasp.
A girl ran to her side. She was wearing
a bright yellow dress and wooden
shoes, which clipped clopped as she
ran.

"This daughter, Rientje."

Rose looked from mother to daughter and noticed that her skin was only slightly lighter than her own.

"I can speak mother... My English is better..." She stopped and looked closer at Rose.

"What clan are you?" her voice inquisitive; her head tilted to one side.

Rose's face once again contorted into a strange bashful look.

"I'm sorry I haven't a clue what you mean..."

The girl came closer and ran her nose

up Rose's arm... "You smell of Wolbear..."

"That was my mother's name..." replied Rose in a quiet voice.

She looked at her "I know!"

*

"The court is in session, the right honourable judge Davis is residing!"

The judge, a thin man with a dusty wig and moth eaten robes cleared his throat and rustled the papers. He looked at the written words in front of

him and then fumbled with his
monocle.

"I see Sergeant, that this man, was
found covered in the blood of the
victim, alas, you found no weapon?"
he momentarily cleared his throat with
the question he just posed to the
policeman.

The courtroom was packed with
Romany's; all holding their breath,
waiting for the next words.

"So Sergeant, what proof have you
that this man is guilty of the murder of
the deceased?" The judge peered
over the paperwork as the monocle
fell away and dangled.

"Well sir... He was well... err... Covered in yon victim's blood your honour..." The policeman was taken aback from such line of questioning from a judge.

The judge merely peered over his paperwork at the Sergeant in the witness stand; intent and enquiring but at the same time daring the officer to step out of line.

That's when Rose noticed a mark on the Judge's hand. It looked to her like Greek lettering...

"And that is enough to sentence a man to death... Is it?" his voice got louder as he went on.

"But sir... He's... A traveller..." the Sergeant began to stumble with his words.

The judge slammed his gavel down. "Are you telling me, SERGEANT." His voice rising to a pitch on the appointment of the officer in the stand. "That this man deserves to die, just because of where he comes from..."

The Sergeant muttered under his breath...

It was obviously enough for the judge. "Bailiff... Get this man out of my courtroom... CASE DISMISSED!"

The Romany's that were crowded
about Rose, rushed into each other's
arms... Except for one man.
He seemed to salute the judge with
one hand.
The judge merely nodded and got
down from his podium.

Rose followed the rabble of happy
Romany's out of the courtroom.

"Rientje..." she called out. She was
the first person that Rose recognised.

Her voice wavered as she looked at
Rose with her head to the side...
"Rose..."

She had a look of seeing Rose in a
complete different way.

"You have no place to call yours?!" Her voice distant.

"I'm sorry... What... how could you know that...?" Rose stammered her words, shocked to hear them from another.

"I can see more about you... And I feel you do to... Would you like a cup of tea?"

Rientje pulled Rose into a cart at the side of the road. Inside sat an old man.

"Rientje iz lovely to zee you!" The thick German accent bellowed out.

"Hi Grampy Wolhawk!" with a smile she climbed in, pulling Rose with her.

The old man stared passed Rientje, his toothy grin and glassy eyes became fixed on the new arrival.
Rientje filled a pot full of water from the kettle and sprinkled in tea leaves from a pot above...

"Hello sir..." Rose couldn't help curtseying

"I am no Sir, young lady... I am a Wolhawk!" he opened his shirt.
Upon his chest she saw a strange mark, like a paw print of a cat.

"This is Rose, Grumpy... She's a

Wolbear..." her voice spritely in the presentation of Rose.

"Really... Zis is interesting..."

Rose leaned forward and placed a hand on his knee.
Just for a moment his eyes started to sharpen... When she took her hand away she saw the glassy look return.

A sigh and a chink signified the tea being poured.

As Rientje turned back to the situation she saw Rose remove her hand from the leg of Grampy and saw the change... "You are a Seer!"

The Clan's origins

Grampy Wolhawk stared at Rose; a smile lighting his face. Rose stood fixed by the gaze of the old man. She felt uneasy at the way the man stared at her. It was as though he were staring into her very soul.

Rientje turned with a cup and saucer in each hand. The room full of tense emotions.

"Please Rose. Sit here, with us. There is much you know not." Rientje didn't quite thrust the saucer into Rose's hands but more directed it skilfully into the unattended hand, the one that had not touched the leg of the old man.

Rose's eyes fell to the fine China cup...
Her lips murmured something
inaudible to the other two in the room.

"Speak up young lady..." Grampy
broke the silence.

"This cup..." Rose uttered quietly.

Rientje cut in. "You have seen
before?"

Rose's eyes perplexed as she
refocused on Rientje.
"My mother's cup..." Rose said in a
haunted voice.

"Zis iz ze identical set made for all clan
leaders..." Grampy's voice speaking as
though in remembrance.

"Then how?" Rose began.

Her mind filling with questions; such as who is she? And who was her mother?

"Sit." the old man held his hand to the bench next to him. "Rientje will explain"

Rientje laid her cup down and joined Rose on the bench.

"There is much to tell." Rientje nervously looked to Grampy for guidance. He merely nodded his head and said. "Everything!"

The caravan seemed to go dark and Rose heard Rientje's voice change, as though speaking with another's voice.

"As far as we know; there were originally thirty-six clans in what was then known as Briton.
We traded with Romans, Saxons and Danes.

Our clans have always dealt in equine; the very best horses.

In the era after the Romans, Briton was a torn country. Many factions rose up and fought amongst each other.
That was until the time of King Arthur. His wisdom and rule allowed safety to all that walked the Kingdom.
His own horse was bought from our Lynx family clan.

The land however fell into darkness and the daughter of Merlin wished to rule instead of Arthur. Whichever way;

she tried to usurp Arthur's reign. His Knights and people stayed loyal to their liege Lord and her attempts from within failed.

Hence, one night, whilst Merlin was on a quest of his own; to bring the standing stones from Eire to this land. Morgana drugged Arthur and raped him in his bed chamber. By the time the guards realised what had happened, Morgana had fled. Arthur had never told Merlin of the betrayal; but in the years to come he found out by his own grandsons lips.

Some sixteen years later; is when the darkness fell once more and Arthur; at his ripe age of thirty-eight, found himself being called to arms against the Saxons; led by his illegitimate heir.

A single clan, the Bear clan. Were called upon to provide as many horses as they could muster and when they realised what was happening they sent their own rider north to inform Merlin.

Merlin was found at a northern stronghold where the castle's occupants were given the gift of living stone.

Together with the Bear clan member he journeyed south to the standing stones. Otherwise known as Stonehenge.

Apparently he had learnt of his daughter's intentions, to overthrow Arthur with a new champion and had been working on a solution.

Hawks, Magpies, Owls, all sorts of birds were called upon to call the clans together.

There at the standing stones the gathering of all thirty-six clans stood. The leaders of each encircled Merlin.

Merlin's speech went something like this.

"Clans of the Earth, Roamers, Romany's. A great evil has spread through the land and I am ashamed, as it is my own blood that has done this"

A murmur ran through the clan leaders.

"You all know of the Nordic Mage's power of the outcast spell... The curse of the Wolf!"

A few leaders went to turn and walk away but others held their arms and bid them to stay a little longer.

"My own daughter, has altered this curse and plans to use an almighty army of wolf men to take control of this Kingdom, you so walk freely in."

Anger erupted from most of the clan leaders some sobbing in disbelief at the thought of an oncoming war.

"What is more, the Wolf curse can be transferred by a single bite or scratch!"

The Magpie clan leader stepped forward.

"And what would you have us do, OH GREAT MERLIN." his tone strong and defiant. Jeering slightly at the news of his daughters conjuring.

A third of the clan leaders stood behind the Magpie leader spurring him on.

"I ask you to fight with me!" As Merlin spoke a dash of lightning struck the ground some twenty leagues away.

The moment those words were uttered, it is said that twenty-four of the clan leaders walked away from the fire pit.

Upon seeing the last of their caravans leave the plains, Merlin spoke once more.

"I am grateful, for you who remain. Can I assume that you are willing to help Arthur and I?" for that one moment, Merlin looked older than the ever.

It was the Hawk clan leader that stepped forward at this moment.

"I speak for all that remain Merlin. You have always been at our aid and it is an honour to be here for you and your King!"

At that moment twelve Druids appeared from the stones surrounding the clan leaders.

Merlin placed hands out. "Be not afraid my friends. The Druids are here to help. I have told you of the true nature of the beast we must now prepare for, for which I also have prepared for."

At Merlin's feet stood a chest plainly crafted from oak. He kicked the lid open and inside; shone silver, stacked to the brim.

"The creatures we face can be killed by silver. There is not enough in all of us to make a difference, so I ask all of your people to take a piece and hold it in their hand!?"

The procession of the Romany's guided by their clan leaders and the

Seers ensured that each one had their piece of silver and in rows the clan members stood.

A cauldron now sat on the open fire, surrounded by the twelve Druids. It bubbled thickly.

Merlin spoke once more.

"To fight a creature we must become its equal. To this end I have concocted a changing spell that will be marked on each of your chests, so that the oncoming battle, you will be better than our enemy."

The Druids and Merlin fanned out to the clans and proceeded to mark the chest and incant a saying that we do *not fully remember.*

One by one the clan members and leaders were led through the standing stones where a bright light emanated from each one.

All had been through, with the exception of the Seers. Merlin stood once more in front of all the clans and explained.

"I have given you all the mark of the Wolfsbane. It is the ability to change into a catlike creature!"

Merlin nodded to the Hawk clan leader, in which he was the first ever, to change into half human half cat. The claws and teeth shone with silver.

"The weakness of the Wolf we face is silver." Merlin spoke aloud.

The Hawk clan leader reared up allowing the silver to reflect the falling sun's rays.

"The original curse was affected by the moon... But my daughter has a helm that can control their change."

The Bear clan leader stepped forward. "Merlin why have you not blessed our Seers?"

"I do not know if there will be adverse effects of your wild magic and I wish no harm to you or your people." He stopped for a moment as though deliberating on a thought.

"Also I must tell you that after our victory, I know some of the wolves may escape the battle for which we head. The mark will be passed down through your children's children. But it will dwindle as I hope you will destroy this threat before the last of you remain."

With that the clans followed Merlin into battle.

*

Rientje came out of her trance state.

 Grampy sat back, his eyes affixed once more on Rose.

Rose lifted the cup to her lips and drank a small sip. The tea was strong and drying in her mouth but she wasn't sure if that was merely the thought on this crazy story she had just heard.

"So..." began Rose. You mean to say that 'We' as a clan hunt Werewolves?"

"Yes..." Rientje's eyes portrayed the look of someone telling the absolute truth.

Rose's eyes turned back to the mark upon Grampy's chest.

"Vot vould make you believe zis story you have heard?" His eyes clearing as though truly seeing.

Rose cleared her throat as though she had a melon within it.

"Well... Grampy... I don't mean to be rude but this seems all so farfetched that... I..."

With this Grampy stood from his chair with a slight wobble.

His face contorted, his jaw line and eyebrows moulding around. His ears rising to the top of head. Hair sprang out from his face.

Rose blinked and as she looked again the old man was gone, and in front of her stood, a stooped golden maned cat, with flecks of grey. The eyes were slits, the teeth bared flashing silver. A huge paw rested upon her shoulder.

"Does zis simplify the matter?"

The Warning in the Leaves

Rose wasn't sure what had happened, between the moment she had seen with her own eyes; the old man known as Grampy Wolhawk, transformed into this mysterious and bizarre creature.

To now; rocking gently in a cot in the back of the caravan.

The midday light shone through. She tried to lift her head but a throbbing feeling, made the room spin.

"Best not to move for now." Rientje's hand rested on her shoulder.

Rose heard a soft tune singing from the front of the caravan.

"It's a long way from Tipperary; it's a long way to go..." The voice was certainly not Grampy Wolhawk's; as the accent was clearly English. Perhaps, a Suffolk accent.

"Where are we?" Rose felt very disorientated from the rocking of the caravan.

"We are going to Essex, Rose. Some of the clans are meeting to discuss the signs." Rientje's voice sounded troubled.

"I'm not sure what you mean..." Rose tried to focus on Rientje.

"Let me pour you another cup of tea..." even with the gentle rock of the caravan; Rientje's movements looked like one of a ballerina. She pivoted this way and that, pouring the tea leaves with one scoop and lifting the old iron kettle from its swing. The water sloshed but not one droplet spilt, as the water danced its way into the ornate teapot.

The sides of the counter had wooden stoppers as the cups slid back and forth.

Rientje leaned forward of the counter and grasped the nearest wooden spoon.

"We need to save a bit of time..." she plunged the spoon into the pot and

stirred vigorously.
She raised the pot and poured
delicately.
Her dance was mesmerising.
The cups chinked and clinked but
stayed upright on their journey.

"Give it a moment to cool; but I know
already the outcome." her eyes
friendly but her face was full of worry.

"Do you mean..." Rose began.

Rientje lifted her hand. "Let's give it a
moment."

They sat in calm silence as the
caravan rocked gently. The sounds
from outside of the gentle clopping of
the draft horse. The whistling from the
driver.

"We should be able to drink now."
Rientje motioned to Rose to drink up.
The tea was harsh with the hint of
Assam.

Finally, drunk to the dregs. The tea
leaves sat heavily on the bottom of
the cup.

Rose upturned the cup into the
saucer.
Rientje watched on in awe. For her,
she had, had to be shown the details
of how to read the leaves. For
instance the water represented the
movement of time; the leaves
represented the ripples, or at least the
burdens that may come to pass.

"It's the same symbol I saw the other
morning." Rose's face quizzical. "It's

the representation of the Wolf?!"

"You amaze me Rose... Did anyone show you this?" Rientje felt she already knew there was something different about Rose.

"No... I haven't ever been shown I've just; known." Rose looked sheepishly at Rientje.

Rientje reached back and pulled a dead rose from a draw.
"I wonder... Please take this... Think of this flower upon its bloom."

Rose took the blackish flaking flower and covered the old dead head in one palm and brought it to her lips. As she did so, the stem changed from brown to green. As her hand opened the head of the rose burst open. The deep red petals were changing, to that of blood red.

"You are remarkable..." Rientje's voice stammered slightly. She took the rose from her grasp and went to the hatch to where the driver sat.

The next moment, Rientje's mother came down the steps.
"Rientje tells me you did..." her hand held the gentle flower. "Who learnt you?"

"She means did someone teach you?" Rientje struggled past her mother who blocked the passage.

"No one. I... Just know..."

Rientje's mother smiled. "Your mother... She die when you born!?" It was like a statement.

Rose's heart ached as she answered. "Yes."

Rientje's mother leapt forward and embraced Rose, in a rib crunching hug. After a little time the embrace softened. Rientje's mother leant back and kissed both cheeks and whispered. "Akuna sa'tei"

Rientje leant in. "it means peace to you soul"

*

It was nightfall by the time the caravan slowed to a halt. Rose peered out of the window and saw trees illuminated by fire.

The doors at the rear opened and the fire's light became more pronounced. The abundant noise from the gathering outside flooded in from the woods.

Rientje and her mother stood at the foot of the steps.
"Come Rose. You have family to see."
The awkward English from Rientje's mother was mixed with delight.

The forest was teeming with an array of different faces. Some like her had darker skin and yet others were pale as the moon or dark skinned as the autumn leaves.

She felt something different about her. Her body felt alive; tingling. It was as though the very air was charged with energy. Oh what she could have done with this energy years back when she had to clean her old house. A pang hit her in the stomach, her father's estate, her only link to the parents that brought her to this world gone and now only a pendant...

Rientje took hold of her hand; it snapped Rose from her daydream. The energy resurged itself.

"You feel it Rose? The spirit?"

Rose felt peace in the shared experience. "What are we feeling?"

"It is the leyline. The vein of energy that flows through our world."

"I feel the energy but I don't understand... What is a leyline?" Rose asked although her voice seemed a hundred miles away.

"All magic is derived from the earth. Our earth mother reminds us when we are close to a vein. She strengthens us... We are the Tovenaar."

Rose felt complete bliss, even more than she had when the old Nanny had died.

Soon Rose started to notice more gruesome details of the crowds she walked through. Some wore necklaces made of animal teeth. A few wore wolf pelts as garments.

She turned to Rientje.
"Why are they..." she pointed to an older man who was surrounded by an eager audience.

"They wear the pelts in pride of victory Rose!"

Rose felt sickened. She had forgotten parts of Grampy Wolhawk's story. Possibly because it seemed so farfetched that her brain linked it too fairies and such like.

"This man Rose, is the Wolbear clan leader... He is your Grandfather!"

Reunion

Rose felt a sharp pang, this time in her chest as her lungs constricted. Anxiety and fear. Her Grandfather?.. She hadn't ever dreamed a day like this day would come. Would she meet his expectations? What did her mother do? Would he hate her for her mother's sins?

Rose stepped back from Rientje's proffered hand. The hand offering to take her to her Grandfather.
Another hand rested on her shoulder. Startled she turned; and there stood Grampy Wolhawk. His kind eyes looking her up and down.
"He von't bite... I promise.." As the

smile broke his aged face, she noticed his teeth had turned to silver and were transformed into the long thin teeth she had once seen before.

Somehow Grampy knew just what to say at the right time. Her lungs relaxed; she could breathe again.

Her Grandfather looked up as though he sensed Grampy.

"BERNE...you old stray... How are you??"

"I am vell villiam... I have a surprise for you!"
With his hand still resting firmly on Rose's shoulder, he pushed her forward.

William blinked a few times; it was as though there was an internal struggle going on behind his eyes. There was happiness mixed with bitterness. She could sense his anxiety flowing from him.

William looked at Rose then to Grampy Wolhawk (Berne) and back again.

"She found us!" Rientje's voice rang out strong from the commotion that was occurring around them, from other members of the other clans greeting each other.

His voice small. "My... Rose?.."

He lunged forward and for a moment Rose thought of running, but Grampy's

hand held her firm.
He threw his arms around her and in her ear; she could hear the soft whimpering of the man's tears.
"You have come home!.."

As he released his embrace of her, he threw up his arms and shouted at the top of his lungs.

"My granddaughter has come home!"

The entire gathering; stopped and looked directly at Rose.

She felt so small; as every eye fell upon her.
William gave a final wave to the cheers that erupted and took Rose off towards a tepee that was erected nearby.

Inside, it reminded Rose of stories of sheikh's tents she had read about. The floor covered in soft carpets. A bed that sat made and ready. The women that were within the tepee. Left nodding to William as though they were servants to him.

Two more men entered with stools and positioned near to the centre.

"Come and sit with me my child..."

The anxiety was back in his voice.

"I'm sorry sir... This is all... Strange"

"You can call me grandpa... My daughter's daughter. Oh how long I have wished to see you and your mother..." he paused waiting for a response.

"She didn't survive my birth...
Grandpa..."
Rose felt awkward delivering this news
as she saw his face drop.

William composed himself, as the
others filed into the tepee.

Rientje and her mother sat beside
Rose. It felt comforting to have them
here with her, even if they were
practically strangers. They were the
closest she had had for friends these
last few days, as any she had been
allowed at her Father's house.

"Rose found us William" it was
Rientje's mother who addressed him.

Grampy Wolhawk, who had just staggered in. "She is Beatrix through and through villiam! More so I vould say."

Rientje excitedly pulled the flower that she had brought back to life from the depths of her clothes. "With no training she managed the renewal..."

William took the rose and turned it in his hands. "If only Beatrix was here to see you..."
More sadness in his eyes deepened the mood of the ones sat around.

A head popped through the tent flap.

"Grandpa... The other clans are only a day's ride away."
On the boys shoulder sat a Raven. It

seemed preoccupied with something until William spoke.

"Thank you Terre and you too Sofia."

He turned to Rose. "Rose this is your cousin Terre Wolraven!"

Terre nodded to her. "I have duties but I'd like to sit and drink with you later cousin!" He smiled and with that he left the tent.

Rose felt strange. Family... She had family. She was no longer alone...

"Sir... Sorry Grandpa... Why is he Wolraven and not Wolbear?"

Grandpa smirked showing long silver teeth. "We are named of our mother's name."

"We are the people of the old ways." a new voice spoke. Entering the doorway stood a woman of six feet in height. Her long hair braided into lots of different strands. Her skin, darker than any of those that sat around the tepee.

"Granddaughter this is Ava Wollynx... Our clan's magi!"

Rose saw the spark within her eyes of one with the gift. Somehow, it was as though a challenge to Rose.

She nodded towards Rose and sat down the other side of William.

"You know Berne, why we are calling this Reid... A new enemy is aligning with our foe."

"I do... Villiam, even your daughter has seen the sign... Do you believe in what some are saying...? Another great war is coming?"

William let his head drop.
"We cannot ignore this one for I believe our enemy will not!"

The Gift of Nature

The very next day; caravans off all
sorts descended upon the commons.
Locals stared from afar with dislike in
their eyes.
So many stories of travellers ruining
land, created a prejudice throughout
the fair country of Britain.
Thankfully, the clans ignored their
stares.

Rose was up early; as was her life
since she was young however she felt
more of a spare part as the women
around her seemed to be doing
everything for her. Apparently the
chief's Granddaughter was treated as
member of the royal family.
Rose threw on her recently cleaned

clothes from the previous day and slipped out of the rear of the tepee before anyone could notice her going.

The birds whistled in the trees and the willow branches seemed to chime with the breath of the wind.
The smell of London was so far behind her; she couldn't think of anything more perfect.
She dipped into the undergrowth. The land fell away sharply and she landed on her bottom.

"Dammit..." she noticed that her clean dress now stained with mud would have to be cleaned again before tonight.

She looked around at the bowl that she now sat within. The tree in the centre seemed higher than any of the others.

The closer she stared, the more the knots resembled an aged face.
She stood, wobbling ever so slightly on her thin shoes and walked slowly with her hand outstretched.

A voice echoed all around her.
"Those are choice words my daughter..."

Rose stood stock still, trembling as she heard the words spoken and yet she could see no one around her.
Gradually she gained confidence, whilst fighting against her stomach cramps.

"Who's there...?" Her voice came out reedy and faint.

She turned around looking at the brush that surrounded the dip of which she stood. Her eyes wanting to focus on the tall tree in front. The leaves seemed to move without the winds interference.

"Don't be afraid... I am father oak..."

The voice seemed more direct this time. She squinted her eyes and the knots in the trees came alive and winked at her. She almost slipped again onto her posterior.

"Father Oak? I'm sorry, I don't

understand..." She wanted to look around for the person who was speaking.

The kindly wooden features of the tree smiled at her.

"Mother and I felt you come into the world, but we had no way of contacting you." a great sigh echoed around and a sadness fell over the face of the tree.

"It was a sad day when your mother passed, but we knew you would find your way back to us!"

So many questions flew around Rose's mind. One found its way to the surface through the haze of random questions.

"What do you mean mother and I? Do you mean my mother?"
Her heart felt as though it were rising into her throat.

The face brightened once again. "Mother Earth, I refer to Rose. Your mother is our daughter as are you... A daughter of the Earth."

Rose felt flabbergasted. She had started to read about different religions in the world, but her Nanny had ripped it from her hands and had thrown the book in the fire. Instead a copy of the Bible was thrust into her hands.

She knew that her abilities to read

leaves were against the teachings of the Bible, but she felt it was right. Her mind; a quandary of questions.

"Time is short o' daughter of mine... We will speak more... For now know this, you are the most gifted of our children; for you will be the broker of peace and the saviour of your people... We love you!"

The face dissolved once more into the wooden trunk and the canopy of the tree opened so that the rays of the sun shone down upon her.

A voice from the far side of the copse called out.
"Rose!"

Rose brushed away tears from her

eyes. She wasn't sure why they were there; but they felt strangely joyful.

The voice called out again and she realised, of whose voice it was from. Rientje.

Rose brushed herself down and climbed back up the side of the bank. As she stretched out her hands, the thin branches came down to her hands and entwined themselves around her slender wrists.

Shocked at their presence she shook them off and lost her footing. Landing once more on the sod.
Her cry of surprise echoed as once more she found herself on the floor. Dirt stains on another side of her dress.

Rientje poked her head through the underbrush.

"What are you doing down there..." Rientje sniggered at the soiled state of Rose's appearance.

"I... Fell..." Rose looked at her wrists as though expecting to see marks from the branches.

"Come... Mother wants to teach us..."

Rose, this time tried running up the embankment, her arms outstretched. Once again the branches reached out and grabbed her wrists. She went to shake them off but this time Rientje shouted at her.

"Don't be afraid Rose!"

The shout was as though a command; she shut her eyes and let the branches pull at her.

She was lifted gently but strongly up the bank and felt her legs dangle in the air. When she opened her eyes, she felt her body descend to the floor. Rientje stood with a look of admiration emblazoned on her face.

"That was amazing..."

Rose watched as the branches released their grasp and went back to their original position.

"What just happened...?" Rose looked

again at her unblemished wrists.

"Mother is going to be amazed... I haven't learnt such as you have done... Mother tells me it takes a long time to do what you have just done" Rientje's mouth was agape.

Rientje took Rose's unprotesting hand and lead her back to the camp.

As the tepees came into sight; women started running over to Rose. They had noticed how dirty she looked. However just as they got close the branches of the trees around them fell down as though to screen them from the pampering hands that reached out.

Rientje pulled Rose around. There

stood Rientje's mother. His hands raised as though mimicking the branches spread.

Her eyes green as the leaves of summer.

"Where have you been?"

Rientje shot a look at Rose. Her eyes told her that she was sent out some time ago.

"I couldn't find her mother..."

"Well you have now!" relief plainly showing on her face.

Rientje's mother's eyes softened, as she looked to Rose. "I am glad that you have been found."

She turned and started walking away. Rientje grabbed Rose's hand and pulled her to follow.

Deeper into the woods they walked. The thrum of the women battling the branches died away.
The trees growing thicker as they walked.

Something felt strange within Rose. A feeling of strength. Her fingers and body thrummed with energy.

Rientje's mother stopped in a small clearing. Willow, hazel, oak and sycamore trees stood sentry around the clearing.

"What is happening?" Rose couldn't help being curious as to the energy that she felt coursing through her body.

Rientje's mother turned and looked at the pair.
"We are at the Leyline. A vein of mother earth's power, which courses through all Tovenaar..."

Rose felt some kind of understanding as to what she meant and yet still it confused her.

Rientje continued
"At a Leyline." She stared intently at them both. "We are strongest. Because our gift is from the earth mother herself."

She closed her eyes and raised her hands above her.

All around the branches of the trees rose above their natural canopy.

Her hands lowered down and with it so did the branches.

In a quiet voice she spoke again.

"Mother Nature cannot be commanded but she can be asked to do as we wish!"

She threw her hands towards the two girls. The branches rushed towards them. Instinctively Rose threw out her hands in defence of the branches rapid approach. The vines and branches encircled around them but not one of the touched the two girls.

Rientje's mother opened her eyes to see the spectacle of the perfect circle in which surrounded the girls.

She dropped her hands and the branches withdrew to their natural hanging.

She walked up to Rose and reached out to Rose's outstretched hands, easing them down.

"You amaze me... From when did you learn this?" Rientje's mother's kind face looked quizzical.

"I...I..."

Rientje spoke up. "That is nothing mother... I saw her this morning..."

Rientje's mother held a hand up to quieten her own daughter.

"You have met him? Please show me what you have learnt!"

It was a request and a command at the same time.

Rose unsure of the events from earlier did as she was bid.

She raised her hands as though she conducting an orchestra and the trees came to life. The branches swayed and swooned flowing and dancing.

The movement of the branches encircled the air; producing noises and gradually creating an enchanting tune. Knocking of wood against wood, the wind passing through hollows and the rustle of leaves.

Tat-tat Tat-tat tat-e-tat Tat-tat... Shh

shh shh-shh-shh... Toot-i-toot toot-i-toot toot-i-toot-i-toot-i-toot...

Gradually Rose lifted her hands to the music and the vines began growing at her feet. Wrapping themselves about her as the merry tune continued to enthral the mother and daughter.

As the music began to fade. Rientje and her mother looking both gleeful and amazed, they began to clap in merriment of the spectacle that had just witnessed.

"I am amazed... Granddaughter!"

Rose turned and behind her stood her grandfather and Grampy Wolhawk. There faces a-mask astonishment.

Rose felt abashed at the attention she was receiving.

"You look as you should... Rose.! Zat is fitting dress for one so gifted!"

Rose looked down on her dress. Although she still wore the soiled dress she had donned that morning, it had been covered by wrappings of ivy and sweetheart.

Her grandfather approached and knelt down before her. Tears flowing in his eyes. He grasped her hand and kissed it gently.

Grampy Wolhawk winked at her then turned to Rientje's mother. "Top zat..."

The Reid, The messenger and the stranger

#Storytellers note :- As some of you may know a Reid, is an old fashioned word used for a gathering at a time of great importance. Such as war or plague.

It was best way for clans or warlords to get there point of view across to aid other parties. That's all I'm going to say for now...#

Three great pyres lit the gathering.

Men and women of different origins sat in wedges of a vast circle. At the point of each segment sat a clan leader.

Rose and her grandfather were the last to walk into the circle.

Murmurs arose, from Rose's attire.

Ava sat waiting for William. Her face unimpressed by Rose's appearance.

William sat next to Ava but in turn asked Rose to sit the opposite side. He smiled at them both.
"Now I feel I am the thorn between two roses..." he laughed out loud and a few that heard, also chuckled.

Grampy Wolhawk stood aided by Rientje.

"You all know vy we are here.. I ask villiam of the ze Wolbear clan to begin

ze Reid!"
Grampy Wolhawk nodded to William and lowered himself back down.

William stood. His face turning from cheerful to grave. It was as though he were about to announce the death of a family member.

"I am sure the rumours have spread throughout our clans; regarding the constant message our Seers have found..." he heaved a deep breath.

 Although William was strong, his years were creeping up on him. He stared around the circle into each of the clans eyes.
He then focused off to his side.
"Bring her!" he roared.

A girl bound both hands and feet. Barely able to stumble, was dragged to the centre of the three pyres. Her body slumped to the ground.

Rose didn't understand. 'What was this wraith of a girl to do with the Wolf in the leaves?'

As she turned to face her grandfather she noticed that he had started his change. She stared past him and noticed others doing the same.

William raised his furry hand and pointed to the fading sun.

"You all know what she is..." his voice rumbled.

The clans now had a ring of the cat like creatures on the inside perimeter. Their eyes slitted, and focused entirely upon the girl.

Rose got up and stood next to her Grandfather, as though to protect the girl from him and from them.
William turned his golden stare upon her.
"Wait..."

Something compelled Rose to ignore his words.
She marched out towards the girl laying hogtied.

She got as far as the inner circle of the fire when the sun dropped below the horizon. A brilliant blue hue covered the trees as the full moon glowed it's brilliance across the night sky.

Rose saw the moon and then looked back to the girl.
Violently she was shaking as though having a fit. Her body warping and twisting. Her scalp, splitting open as though it were crudely being pulled apart by the ends of her hair.

She rolled this way and that. Gradually the ropes that held her snapped under the tremendous pressure her own body was placing upon them.
Almost silently Rose could hear her screaming, wishing that it would stop.
Tears rolled down her cheeks as

mouth and nose seemed to turn inside out and began to sprout hair.

Behind Rose, William went to step forward but Ava held him fast.

The girl now taller and yet hunched stood free from the bonds that had held her. The face growing hair all over; the sickening look of flesh being ripped at the mouth and nose.
The beast turned and stared right into Rose's eyes.

Its head arched back and a howl echoed from the long snout. As though to call brothers and sisters to arms.
Rose placed her hands in front of her.
'What was she thinking?'

The beast in front of her. Whence was just but a little girl: It affixed it's stare upon Rose.

There they stood as Rose and the beast; sized each other up.

A cloud passed in front of the moon. Rose expected the beast to transform back. However the beast remained. Spittle now dribbled down its long chin. It was eyeing up its prey.

Rose looked deeper into the eyes of the creature before her. Sadness, loss, pain, longing....

Something strange happened next. It was as though that little girl was trapped within the Wolf's eyes; and that she saw her staring from within a tunnel pleading and crying whilst the animal wanted to rip her limb from limb.

Rose took a step forward, passed the line of the three pyres triangle.
The Wolf to everyone else snarled and spat, whereas for Rose, she could hear the cries from within.
Another pace forward and the beast lashed out. Narrowly missing Rose's face.
More determined than ever Rose pushed forward. Her hands palms outward and down by her hips.
The Wolf lashed out again but this time it only got half way.
A vine from the ground had wrapped itself about clawed paw.
Another step, another swipe. Once

more missing its mark and being held. The vine wrapped about the Wolf's body ensnaring and calming the creatures violent wanting.

It was brought to its knees as Rose got so close that she was being showered in the spittle that blew from its wrapped muzzle.

She placed her hands either side of the Wolf's head. Staring deeply into the eyes of the once child.

Rose closed her eyes and rested her head upon its head.

Within her mind she could see herself looking face to face with the scared little girl.

"Please I don't understand what is going on." said the voice of the little

girl.

"It's ok. You won't hurt me." Said Rose

Another voice interrupted. "She won't hurt you but I will ..." the gruff voice of the wolf spat hatred.

It tried to get closer but as it did the wolf was dragged flat to the ground within the vision.

"Please I killed my family. I couldn't stop it..." the petrified girl called out.

Rose went over and pulled the little girl into a hug.

Rose released her grasp and walked over to the wolf's form that now lay on the ground, wrapped tight.

"It's not your fault..." Rose's eyes rounded on the wolf creature now pinned to the floor. "It's his!"

The little girl looked slightly relieved.

"Why are you here?" Rose placed a foot on the back of the wolf.

"Isn't that obvious daughter of the great chief? I'm here to kill you!"

In that moment a flash of images rose into Rose's mind.

A red flag with a swastika symbol. Men marching in grey uniforms with rifles on their shoulders. A man on a platform his hand held like he were brushing dirt from his shoulder.

The man behind him. An evil smile

lingered on his lips. On his tunic sat badge in the shape of the wolf's head in the tea leaves.

Then back to the men marching. Only this time there not men but wolves. They've all stopped and now there staring at Rose.

At once they lunge forward.

Rose was knocked backwards past the line of the pyres lit.

Soundly she realised the bounds of the vines had come loose and the wolf had knocked to the ground. She looked up and saw the hunkering beast lumbering toward her. Its eyes full of malice and intent of destroying. Not caring that its demise was just past the fires, only caring that it would at least take one mortal soul with it.

As it went to leap, mid-way its facial expression changed to one that was caught by surprise. An arrowhead protruding from its chest to where the heart would be. It fell on top of Rose.

Rose raised her head and saw the little girl inside. This time she was no longer afraid, moreover she was thanking her.

The clans were up on their feet looking for the archer. Mixed emotions running high. How dare they take their prey, but thanking as they saved the Granddaughter of the chief.

Rose pulled herself from the slain

body of the wolf girl. Gradually and shakily got to her feet.

From the darkness of the woods stepped a tall figure. In one hand sat a carved wooden bow. The other was raised; palm facing outward as though to say that it came in peace.

Low grumbles from the surrounding cat men were quieted by their clan leaders.

The Seers however all seemed to be on their guard.

"Approach Fayrie... and state your business!" William's voice echoed off the trees.

The figure walked into the centre of

the pyre and deftly pulled the shot arrow from the corpse of the wolf.

Then with one swift motion, it slid the arrow into its hold, pulled the bow over its shoulder and lowered its hood.

He stood there. The one they called a Fayre. Rose was enthralled the moment she looked upon him. He was handsome, sculpted and alluring. His eyes strange as he looked around at those present.

"I will only ask once more Fayre. What is your business here?" William commanded an answer. His hand high in the air.

Somehow Rose felt that if his hand where to fall, then something bad would happen.

"My name is Pasquaile. And I have a message from my mother Danu!" His voice calm, almost serene.

"And to whom is this message for, Fayrie?" spat Ava.

The Fayrie raised his slender hand and pointed directly to Rose.

The Land Underwater

Rose was taken from the pyres to her grandfather's tepee.

The Reid. Disbanded for the night; the clans calming after a shocking evenings affairs.

"I don't know what he wants with her except what the damn Fayries always want with humans..." Williams's voice carried from five tepees away.

Rose looked to Rientje.

"What am I missing..." Rose looked pleadingly at her friend about what was going on and why her grandfather would be so upset about.

"This is no time to be acting rashly William." The voice heavy in an African accent.

"He iz right Villiam. Ze Fayre have not come to zis realm to talk since before Arthur's war!" Grampy Wolhawk's voice unmistakeable.

Heavy footsteps outside the tepee suggested that they had arrived to see Rose.

Rientje went to go, but Rose held her hand firm. Her eyes pleading not to leave her.

She nodded and sat back down.

William marched into the tent. Shortly followed by a large muscular black man and Grampy Wolhawk.

"Asha, how can I not act rashly?" William turned and stared directly at his Granddaughter.

"And you! What were you thinking?!" William's finger pointed directly at Rose.

Rose looked up at her Grandfather. He had not seen what she had seen. The little girl in the tunnel. Haunted by the wolf and his actions, nor the oncoming devastation. She returned his glare with pure defiance in her eyes.

William's finger began to shake. Even Grampy Wolhawk seemed to be shaking.

#Asha means life in Swahili#

They both burst into laughter.

"My goodness granddaughter. You look like your mother when you look like that!"

Asha, Grampy Wolhawk and William her Grandfather formed a seated circle about her.

A commotion from behind the tent flap signalled another arrival.

Ava was launched through the flap into Asha's waiting hands. In walked Rientje's mother. Her eyes pure green.

"DON'T YOU DARE WILLIAM!"

They all turned and looked toward the infuriated Tovenaar.

When she surveyed the room she went almost bashful.

"I promise you my Dutch Tulip; I have no wish to harm either of these girls." He turned sideways as though speaking with Grampy Wolhawk. "And I like my bulbs were they are..."

The men all sniggered.

"Grandpa..." Rose looked toward him. "I know what the leaves are saying!"

Rose recanted the vision she saw within the mind of the wolf. How the red flag flew and the marching soldiers turned to wolves and lunged for her.

Gradually William called out for other Clan leaders and Seers to join them and soon Rose had spoken the same story four times over.

Outside the tepee, the birds started to tweet their morning song.

"William." a dark haired man spoke out.

"Yes Michael?" William held his hand out for the others to silence their bickering.

"What is this Fayre doing amongst us? Why now?" His hands opened and closed like a bible on a Sunday.

William stared about the others

around him. He screwed up his face in thought and then let out an enormous yawn.

"My friends. We have spoken till the morning's dawn. Let us rest on the things we have learnt and meet once more tonight!"

*

Rose fell into a fitful sleep. The furs that encompassed her tickled with their pockets of warm air.

"Rose..."

"Rose, can you hear me?"

*"**Who are you?**"*

"I am Pasquaile... My mother sent me. For you!"

*"**But why me I don't understand...**"*

"You already know..."

The darkness returned and within the folds of her sleep she revisited the visions over again.

*

When Rose awoke the tent was still. The sunlight failing, and the flickering of the re-built pyres began there dance on the outer shell.

She pulled herself up from the wrappings of her slumber and pulled on a fresh dress that had been laid out for her.

Stepping out from the tent flap she bumped directly into Terre.

"I'm sorry cousin. Grandfather sent me for you!" Terre seemed taller today as though his responsibilities were higher.

Together they walked toward the glowing warmth.

The clans noisy at first, but as she got nearer they all became silent. Whether in awe or in fear.

Rose stood next to her Grandfather.

He turned to her. "It's time we find out what these Fayre want with you!" his eyebrows raised.

His voice clear and loud. "Come forward herald, Tuatha De Danann!"

Through the flickering flames, Rose saw the effortless silky movement of the fayre. This time however he presented no weapon. About his wrist laid vine shaped jewellery.

"William Clan Leader of the Wolfsbane Bear Clan." With this he seemed to bow slightly in acknowledgement. "I have been asked to bring your granddaughter to my mother. Danu!"

A growl erupted from one side.

"And why doesn't the old witch come herself?" this time it was Michael. The dark haired man who spoke earlier that day.

Pasquaile seemed to brush off the insult as though it were a mosquito.

William glared at Michael for a moment. "My friend has a good point. Why does Danu, not come herself?"

Pasquaile seemed to take a moment. Then he reached behind his back and pulled out a bottle of liquid. Almost ceremonially, he walked forward and poured the liquid into a bowl that sat in front of Ava.

All eyes seemed to be drawn to the water that had been poured into the bowl.

Gradually like water being forced from a spring underground. It rose, higher and higher until it formed a woman's shape.

"William, Berne... Ah... you." The liquid figure stopped and looked upon Michael.

Michael was on his feet, silver claws sprouted at the ready.

If it weren't for the swift actions of his fellow clansmen, Rose felt he would have been soaked head to foot.

"Vy Danu. You see he iz upset from the last time your people came to his settling!" Grampy Wolhawk looked at the watery figure abhorrently.

"Simple Berne. You know what is coming. I push for a truce and an alliance..." she paused.

"Alliance... With this thing?" Michael still struggled against the bounds of his brothers.

"Send the girl and we will talk... Don't; then I'll speak with the other parties...!"

The water seemed to instantly circum to gravity and land back in the bowl without a droplet out of place.

Murmurs ran through the clans like wildfire through dry brush.

So far they knew of the threat behind the red flag, but curiosity ran rife as to why the queen of the Fayre would seek audience with the lost granddaughter of the Wolbears.

Rose turned towards them all. "I will do it...!" internal conflict ran through as she couldn't understand where the fear came from.

William turned to her. "I shall not stop you granddaughter, but heed this. Drink nothing they give you, eat nothing they hand you and take nothing that is gifted to you!" His eyes fearful.

She nodded to him in acceptance of the terms.

"I want an assurance she will come back within one of our days, in the same mind and heart that she is now!" William almost butted heads with the Fayre who had been the messenger.

Pasquaile stepped back from him and waved to the trees. Another figure walked from the shadows.

"This is my sister Brigit. She has volunteered to be here whilst Rose confides with us." Pasquaile's hand brushed the hood from his sister's head. It fell away showing long red hair.

William pulled Rose to him. "I don't

want to lose you again, oh daughter's daughter of mine. Come back soon!"

Pasquaile led Rose away from the throng of the fires, deeper into the darkness of the trees.

It was strange as the light of the fires diminished. The pale blue of the moon illuminated the path ahead.

"Please join me here." Pasquaile had walked down into a stream, his slender hand held out.

Rose slid her hand in, whilst feeling the water fill her shoes. "What now?" she asked cheekily feeling silly to have stepped into a stream in the dead of night.

"Hold your breath…"

The next moment; the world seemed to turn upside down and round again. As though she gone for dive into a lake and yet ended up dry the other side.

"Where…" began Rose.

Danu in her full form stood surrounded by at least ten others. "You are in the Grove of the Fayre, Rose. Or as your people once called it the land under the water…"

Alliances, Truces and History

Trees moved without wind, light came from everywhere and yet nowhere. Peaceful and serene.

Rose stared at the Queen of the Fayre. In return she stared back. Each one seeming to measure the other.

Pasquaile shuffled his feet impatiently. "Perhaps our guest would like to see some of our home before we get to the matter at hand?" he said hesitantly.

Danu smiled; her teeth, odd looking in the light.

Pasquaile took Rose's hand and lead her away toward what seemed to be the heart of the grove.

Once they were out of earshot Rose got closer to Pasquaile.

"She is really your mother... "Rose felt as a giddy as a binkying rabbit in spring. She couldn't believe that she was in another land. Constantly she blinked taking in the colours, subtle but amazing.

"Yes she is my mother. But also our Matriarch." said Pasquaile in a hushed voice.

"You mean like elephants?" Rose looked closer into his eyes. They seemed to be calculating the answer.

Finally he nodded to her. "Yes exactly like your term for a Mother Elephant that leads the herd. Except hours carries more weight!" A smirk broadened his lips.

Rose smiled back slightly abashed by the smile he was giving her.

A sheet as fine as silk draped between two large trees, parted as they got near. A large clearing, with hewn wooden tables and strange goblets and plates sat with an arrayment of different dishes.

Pasquaile followed Rose in, staring at the expression on her face. "You are welcome to any of this food Rose!"

Rose felt her stomach rumble but

heard the words spoken before she had agreed to follow down the waterway.

"I had best not." her stomach rumbled once more. This time Pasquaile looked at her with piercing green eyes. Rose stopped for a second. His eyes had been brown before. Her head felt slightly woozy, as though a fog had passed over her. In the back of her mind she heard herself. **'Rose wake up...'**

Rose suddenly cleared the fog and as she looked down she saw sweet cake in her hand. She dropped it to the floor.

She stared once more at her hand and then rounded on Pasquaile. Her hands stretched to the floor; ivy shooting out of the ground.

"Don't you ever try that again!" She growled. The ivy wrapped all around him until it was up till his neck.

"Well done!" Danu walked up behind Rose, placing a hand on her shoulder and then leaning in and pulling her into an embrace. "Now we can talk!"

Danu and Rose walked hand in hand through into a long room with a throne made of roots. Pasquaile and Danu's minions followed behind them.

The tapestries on the walls showed images of the man on the stand. His hand in the position of holding a waiter's tray. Another full of a wolf pack running through woods with blood splattering in their wake.

Danu waved her hand by her throne and a second chair grew out of nowhere.

"Sit, child of Wolbear" She looked around at her minions. "This child cannot be bound by our magic." Her eyes fell upon her son. "Should you try then she has my permission to do as she sees fit!"

Rose saw some small Adam's apples gulp and bob.

Danu raised a hand and a sheet draped down, separating them from her minions.

"I can see so many questions flying about Rose. Let's see where I can answer some of them." Danu's hand pointed back to the sheets.

A small spider seemed to edge its way to the middle, gradually it went round and round the web changing colours, until a picture starting forming.

Danu's voice seemed to come from the background.

Our history begins before the start of man. Before the earth was given form. We came from across the ocean of stars searching a new world on our ships of light.

Rose saw long Viking style ships

sailing across the vast blackness of space.

When earth was formed we found a paradise. The inhabitants were reptiles, beautiful and strong. They left us alone and in turn we did the same. We as a people decided to make this our new home.

Peace reigned for many years. Until the time, of the rain of fire.

Our ships exploded into flames leaving us stranded on this land.

Our only option was to find a land within this land. My love died finding the Grove. He was supposed to follow us in...

The image changed and warped to later in the years. Man had entered the land, he ran about with Iron and Bronze weapons.

By this time our people had come to call the Grove their home. But alas living in the Grove had its effect on us. No longer in the light our bodies became infertile. Our race, were dying.

The humans thought of us as gods or demons. They either wanted to worship us or kill us.

The first human - Fayre child grew strong and well. Even though the half breed had a lesser life it gave us a chance to survive. But it came at cost.

As soon as they were introduced to our magic they were overcome with the fog. Losing their free will.

Women and men walked without purpose.

Some of those more recently affected, sadly were members of the Wolfox clan.

We tried to limit the visits to your world. Only to try and re-populate our own. That was until your world re-entered ours.

The last time humans entered our lands was in the form of a young woman, by the name of Morgana.

She was one of the first to resist our

magic. Unusually talented in the lore's of a mage; she approached me direct and asked for an alliance.

I offered her a choice. If she bore a child without defect then she would have our alliance on the war she wished to rage.

She bore a son but something was wrong. Her son was born of the blood eye. A powerful hate resided within him, by the time he came of age he was nothing more than a wraith.

I then saw where the hate resided. His mother carried it like a torch. Fuelling her hatred from within. Driving her.

When I told her that her offspring was not suitable she raised fire within the grove.

Burning trees and silken sheets to ash. Danu's face grave with the damage to her home.

I sent her away from this place although she left such a mark on us that we have never forgotten her hatred.

Merlin her father was the next to enter our realm. He did not offer to sire nor did he try to appease me. Instead he showed me the world beyond our grove should we not act.

It was the last time my bow was used to kill a mortal.

A silver birch bow and a single ornate

arrow hung from her form in the web.

As the image faded, the spider dropped to the floor and scurried away.

"Now you see Rose Wolbear. I know what you have seen for I have seen as well. In the tapestries of the passing. It is time I offer the aid to **You!**"

Preparation For War

The Reid's third night was one of a mixture sadness and tension.

With the return of his Granddaughter. William embraced Rose so hard she felt her breath leave her.

Pasquaile stood back from the others conversing with his sister.

Grampy Wolhawk pulled Rose into another bear hug and then rounded on the trio of fires.

"Rose Wolbear has done things I thought not possible. Zis is an amazing day!" His voice loud and confident.

A susurration of muttering swept over those gathered.

William his face sullen; his voice deep and commanding. "Although we have news of an alliance. We must also face that there is a war coming. One we have not faced in our lifetime!" William stopped and placed a hand on Grampy Wolhawk's shoulder as though the weight of what he must say next would be too much without the strength of his friend. "We will need to prepare, to protect this world from the wolf. From those that will do us harm!"

A roar went up round them. Each clan member stood there hands to their chest.

William turned to Rose. "Well Granddaughter, I hope you are ready"

Rose looked him in the eyes. "Grandpa, we will do what must be done…!" She winked and led him back to the tent.

*

Messengers were sent out to those that had not been able to attend the Reid.

Meanwhile the clan leaders spent their time grouping there best fighters. Both those with the mark, seers and those wishing to fight.

Rose walked amongst the camp hearing the different accents and languages present. Rientje had taken to be her guide whenever her mother allowed her to be.

She stopped at the edge of a clearing. Men and Women stood side by side with long silver spears. Practicing there lunges and defences. The marked in their cat form played like kittens almost. Pouncing on each other. Taking each other to the floor by the throat. Grouping up and attacking a smaller group.

To the side young girls, some younger than her; watched and listened to an older seer.

She watched with wonder as a little

girl tried her utmost to pull the vines from the earth. The seer barked at her and she fled with tears in her eyes.

Rose ran after her.

Deeper in the woods she went and soon Rose found it harder and harder to follow.

She closed her eyes and stretched out with her mind. The woods allowed her to see the little girl throwing herself into tree's hollow. Her dark hair flomping over her hands and knees as the girl sat there and sobbed.

Rose stepped up on top of the fallen tree and walked until she reached the roots reaching to the sky.

"Are you ok?!"

"Pardon Mademoiselle, J'en comprend pas…" She sniffed noisily.

Rose was at a loss. She had not been any good at languages. She shrugged shoulders. "I'm sorry I don't know any French."

A large golden coloured marked cat jumped over the fallen tree, landing next to Rose.

"She does not understand" the low purring voice emanated from the feline in front of her.

It changed into its human form; it was Terre.

He turned to the girl and spurted

words so fast that she barely heard the start and stop of the words. In return she spoke with same vehemence.

"She said she wishes she was like you." said Terre

Rose looked between them. "You can speak French?" asked Rose.

"All the marked can Cousin. Something to do with the spell that was used..."

*

"Winston is a good man. He warned the order that this would happen!"

"But he's not in favour at the moment."

"I can think of no one better than Major Winston Churchill to lead this country. Chamberlains stance won't work."

Rose coughed before she entered.

In front of her stood her grandfather and the same man from the trial

"Ah Rose... this is Father David." William proffered his hands to the man he had been speaking to.

"It is my pleasure to meet you; I believe I saw you at the trial..." said Father David

William cut in. "Father David is from

the order of Ezekiel. Like us they are concerned for the events that are unfolding. His order have great sway with governments..."

Father David looked towards William. "I think William that we can dispense with any more talk of business tonight. Enjoy your evening!" father David tipped his head towards Rose and walked out into the night air.

Rose looked astonished at her grandfather. "Who?"

"The order of Ezekiel, granddaughter." he shook his head. "Have you read the Bible? Koran? The Tanakh?"

"I have read some of the Bible but I don't recall the name."

"The prophet Ezekiel was the first prophet in the new religions to state that there is evil in this world."

"Why do they come to us?" Rose looked astonished.

"We Wolbear's have forged an alliance with the order." William at down on his chair and patted the adjacent to his.

"For many years, our ancestors defended themselves against these new religions. There wanting for blood and silver has always been strong." he sighed. "There came a time when they realised that there was a greater threat to themselves from the werewolves. An emissary from the Vatican held out an olive branch to us and from then on we have been allies."

"What are these other evils you speak of father? "Rose sitting by her grandfather feeling aghast at the thought of more evil.

"Demons granddaughter; with black wings, human form and teeth sharp enough to be mosquitoes noses." he smiled a toothy smile, one shining of silver. "I think I shall tell you more in the morning."

That night Rose dreamt of horrifying scenes of carnage, blood soaked halls and bodies a wash on the floor; drained of their life's blood.

First wave

The year was 1938. Ships crossed the oceans carrying Jewish refugees. Hate was driving then from their homes. Even the new homes they were escaping to were not sure if they wanted them.

Midst these crossings, a return journey took a number of caravans, horses and Romany gypsies.

Rose sat on the swaying ship between England and France her head hung over the rails. She lifted it temporarily: "I can't see why we couldn't have travelled the way the Fayre do. Oh ooo..." another torrent of bile erupted from her.

"I told you cousin, they want everything their way. They say they are here to help us but I'm not sure anymore." Terre swigged a small bottle of beer. "It is nice to have first class all to ourselves, well that is if you can get your head up from the side long enough."

The crossing for Rose felt like the longest two hours she had ever known. It had not helped that on top of the rocking and the diesel fumes; the vibration of the engine and pounding noise threw out all of here senses. What she wouldn't give to be back ashore, to feel the grass between her toes, the smell of the pollen or even just feel of the rocking of free caravan.

*

Rose practically threw herself on the ground as she got out as the others calmed the horses and withdrew the caravans.

Cars drove on the opposite side of the road. Rose stared as to local men seemed to squabble about who was first in the queue to board the boat.

"What is happening?" Rose asked.

"They're leaving cousin. It is clearer now to them than before of the evil that is coming"

He was right; this was not just French or German or Austrian that were leaving Europe. It was Polish and Czech.

The troop of caravans began their journey towards the East.

There were ten caravans in procession. Each one carrying at least five people. Three seers, fifteen marked and the rest, those willing to fight.

Rose stood in the back with the other two seers. Making tea and talking.

"He is very handsome, and he's a marked." Gertrude blushed as she spoke. She was the most inexperienced of the three.

"Oh Gerty, when are you going to learn. These marked don't want to settle down."

Rose stared at Erin in shock. "Why forever not... Gerty is very pretty and I see the way he blushes around her."

Erin scoffed at Rose "Like you would know all our ways..."

Gertrude slapped Erin's leg hard enough to silence the room for a moment.

She then rounded and stared at Erin. "We are here to help Rose learn all of our ways Erin. You know that!"

"Ok then, what is the first rule of the clans?" Erin's eyes piercing green, stared at Gertrude.

In a solemn voice she spoke. "Clan before all other!"

"Grandfather said that the moment the thirty six clans split ways at the time of the blessing. The twelve remaining clan's leaders set this in place around the standing stones." Rose interjected, attempting to bring calm to the caravan.

The caravan's wheel hit a rut and Rose was thrown forward. Erin rose to catch her before she fell into the stove.

"Thank you." Rose smiled.

Erin startled to chuckle. "I hope this will be returned someday..." She winked back at Rose.

The girls prepared tea, sat on the cot, come bench and read their leaves in sequence. Each staring over each other's shoulders.

"I just don't understand. The leaves have never been this hard to read." Gertrude's voice unnerving.

"I spoke with Seer Ava. She said that this can happen closer to a time of uncertainty..." Her voice was unsure as to whether she was sure of what she was saying.

"I had this once before." The girls turned and looked at Rose. "It was back when I knew nothing of who I was..." her voice went quiet.

The two girls each put an arm about her. Rose had only just realised that with everything that had happened, she had not had time to reflect. The Nanny, the werewolf, the Queen of the Fayre and now War.

*

"We are coming close to the German border. Keep silent and let us do the talking!" A voice called from the caravans hatch.

Indistinct voices

"Hallo Mein Herr!"

"Vos ist dies? Halt Wohnwagen und ihre papiere!"

"Ja ist good"

"Danke, Auf Wiedersehen!"

The caravan started rumbling again along the road.

The hatch opened and Terre walked down the steps. Gertrude's face went bright red.

"We're going straight across Germany if we can ladies..." his eyes cast across Gertrude's and he blushed. "Erm... you see the Nazis are rounding up Jews and Romany's, but thankfully the border guard was a friend."

Erin's eyes turned bright green. "You

are friends with a Nazi?"

"If it weren't for that friend, we would be either turned away or imprisoned right now…" Gertrude's eyes had gone the same colour.

Rose looked at Terre and smirked. She raised her hands above the two girls, and covered them in ivy.

"Now listen you two. Terre is my cousin. You can fight over him, after we have found out what the wolves are doing…" She pulled her hands down and made them both sit on the bench.

The leaves rescinded back to the wooden surround of the caravan.

"Cousin, my friend slipped me this note with my papers." said Terre

Rose opened the folded letter.

My Dearest Friend

I have done everything I can to make sure you travel is safe. I'm not sure how long I will be able to stay. They are hunting us.

The word coming through from our friends in the order; is that the wolves have a new weapon which they aim to use against all of mankind.

Zwiesel. Make your way there.

✡ ☐ Ω ∞

D.A.R.

Rose looked at Terre. "A new weapon certainly explains the visions of what we have seen. What is the meaning of D-A-R?"

"Its 'destroy after reading' cousin" Terre smiled at Rose. It was a sad smile.

*

The travel across Germany was long and arduous. The wheels on two of the caravans meant that they all had to squeeze into the other eight.

Snow began to cover the roads and soon many of the occupants had to help the horses in pushing the caravans up the hills.

"I wish it wasn't so cold..."Gertrude's eyes flicked to Terre's.

Rose knew what they were thinking, somehow it warmed her to see them happy in there uncomfortable love they had.

"I'm sure Terre will keep you warm young Tovenaar..." Another boy touched with the mark interrupted.

"Thanks Boet. I shall remember to ice bath you before you wake!" Laughter erupted from them.

"Come on younglings. We need to reach the outskirts of the town tonight!" Asha had journeyed with them as the head of the expedition. Unlike the others, it was plain to see the wolf furs under his heavy hessian cloak.

The grunts and groans of the party moved ever on.

*

From a far hillside sat two people. A Nazi officer and a scruffy unclean man.

"I told you, cap-i-tan... you have a leak in the company you keep."

"Zis means nothing. We will destroy them."

The other man lifted his nose to the air. "I smell at least ten with the mark... and something else. You are best to leave this to me and my kind."

"Zis is my command. Herr Reilly. I vont my men to have first-hand experience in killing these vermin!"

"Very well, then my men lead yours to teach them how to eat well!"

*

Finally by the time dusk started to fall

the caravan had made the outskirts of the small village of Zwiesel.

Through the darkness, the lights of the community below shone warmth and welcome.

"Terre. Take Rose to town with you tonight. You will be less conspicuous if you travel as a couple to the inn!" Asha said as he loaded the stove with logs.

Gertrude looked to Rose and then back to Terre.

"Surely Asha, I should take Gerty...!"

"No… I want you both back safe and sound. You are more likely to do something stupid when you are in love with someone!"

Terre and Gertrude both started shuffling their feet.

"Of course I've known for a while. You two are just too stupid to admit it." He let out a large booming laugh.

Rose walked up to Gertrude. "I will bring him back to you I promise!"

The air bit as the door opened. The temperature was falling fast.

Rose and Terre walked arm in arm toward the glowing lights.

*

"Guten Abend!" Terre looked at the barman.

The barman looked angry as he looked at Terre.

Rose looked behind the bar. There behind him sat a number of mini flags. It seemed everyone was there except for the swastika.

She took a chance. "I beg your pardon kind sir. Could we have something to take the chill off?"

At the words spoken the barman puffed out his chest. "English?"

Terre looked to Rose. What was she thinking?

The barman leaned across the bar, grabbed Rose's face in a lock and pulled her across the bar virtually. A rough kiss on both cheeks then she was placed gently back on the floor.

"Welcome to my inn! It so great to have you hear!"

Soon a number of locals had flocked around them as though they were an attraction.

"I'm sorry I don't understand?!" As Rose was handed a glass of Jägermeister.

"Zis will take the chill from your bones young one.!" Said a bearded local.

"Mein Dames. We are not German. We

are BAVARIAN!" a chant went up through the entire inn.

"ACHTUNG!"

"Quick go with Karl. Bad men are coming!"

Rose and Terre were rushed below into the cellar, the lid to the cellar shut quietly and that is when they heard the arrival.

"Ah Bartender, would yee get me men, some of that lovely liquor, you got flowing over there.!"

Another man walked in behind them. His boots stamping officially on the floor.

"It iz good you are so velkoming Karl!"

"Danke mein herr." His voice calm and servile.

"You haven't had any visitors tonight now have you...?"

"Nein mein herr!" his voice keeping its low tone.

"Good, und you can speak in English this night; to celebrate our friends who have joined the Third Reich!"

"Jawhohl mein herr..."

A voice from across the bar spoke up. "Why does the Fuhrer chase Jews?" The man looked worse for wear.

"Ah Christophe isn't it. Yes the Fuhrer has decided that we should know who are Jews are, so we need not drink beer with them." His voice jeering.

"The Fuhrer is half Jew. He should chase himsel…"

BANG

Smoke curled from the end of the Luger. "Zis man was a traitor to the Fuhrer. His lies will die with him!"

Down in the cellar; another hatch opened.

"Psst. Com ist." it was but a whisper.

A woman waved at the pair join her.

Strangely the room below the cellar seemed larger.

Behind them a panel slid back,

seamlessly covering any trace of it being there.

"You must be Terre. The names Charles. British intelligence." his hand stretched out in front of him.

Terre looked him up and down with suspicion. Whereas Rose grasped his hand firmly and looked into his eyes.

"It's alright Terre, we can trust him enough." Rose still locked into his eyes and speaking sideways.

"Sorry about the debacle up there old Adolf has a thing about hiring thugs to do his dirty work. All intents and purposes though it seems to have won enough of them over, the rest are all too bloody scared."

Rose looked to the man who seemed to be joking with the death of a man who was clearly grieving.

"Sorry bad taste was it. I'm afraid this is being more of a daily occurrence... ermmm... yes why you're here. "He fumbled with a small pile of papers and pulled out a folder, on it were the words. 'Wolf wache'

A picture fell out. The picture showed a transformation in progress of human to werewolf.

"I'm sorry if this is disturbing miss." Charles went to take the photo away but Rose held fast onto it.

In the background something seemed odd. Normally when people are the transformation there is fear on a person's face but the other man in the photo wasn't just smiling, he was ecstatic.

"Who is this man? "Rose's finger fell on the man in the picture.

"We're not sure. All we know is that he comes from Scandinavia. Bit of lunatic that one. Loves watching the change. "Charlie handed out some other photos.

Yet again, there he was. Almost jumping up and down with gay-full glee.

Terre broke Rose's concentration. "Where is there base Charles? We need a better look!"

"Here near to the border with the Czech Republic. I'm sure that's why German forces have already invaded under the pretence of securing their border." Charlie finger pointing to the Bayerischer Wald.

"Thanks Charlie; now is there another way out?" smiled Terre.

Charlie showed Rose and Terre another hatch that lead to tunnel that would emerge two houses away from the inn.

The walk back to the caravans was one of paranoia and suspicion in case they were followed.

By the next morning the caravans were on the move again towards the border.

*

A handful of men stayed with the wagons, the others split up in search of the base of the Wolf Wache.

Rose had volunteered to go with the group lead by Asha. Terre and Erin went off with another. Gertrude although uneasy went with Boet.

The snow seemed to be deeper with every step. Asha and the other marked had changed to their catlike form as to tread easier on powder.

Rose grabbed a branch from a nearby tree. The evergreen spanned out like hand. She placed it on the floor and let fresh vines bind them to her feet.

As they walked something felt strange to Rose.

"Is everything OK Rose? " Asha was looking at Rose in a bizarre way.

"There's a Leyline nearby…" She said in calm voice.

"I smell wet dog…" purred another.

"We must be getting close. Rose can you leave a marker so that we know where to return tonight." purred Asha.

Rose leant down into the snow, her hands cupped. She whispered into her hands. Out grew a shoot of green leaves and then a bud.

"It will Bloom when I return Asha." her voice confident as she stepped back.

They walked back to the caravans; a raven flew off to the other groups.

*

Night came and as the half-moon rose; Asha stood in front of all of those that had come.

"Tonight we face our enemy and our

enemy's new ally. They are ruthless as we must be. There can be no survivors!" Asha's eyes changed as he spoke and his voice growled on the last word.

Terre leant into Rose. "Grandfather told me that anything happens to you, then he's going to castrate me..." he chuckled solemnly.

They separated once more, however this time Terre stuck with Rose and Asha took Gertrude.

The crunch of the snow under foot, crackled loudly in the air. The wind rustled the branches leaving tensions high.

The rose bush began to blossom as

Rose got closer. Its colour's somehow shone with the Moonlight.

Rose spread her hands back to stop the party she was with.

"Something is wrong. The flower is tainted..." whispered Rose.

"How can that be? You planted it only this morning..." Asked Terre

"I don't know..."

A sound like buzzing bee flew through the air. Another flew past and knocked the man behind Rose to his back. His eyes staring up to the moon's half glow.

Terre changed into his Cat form and pounced upon Rose. Meanwhile he growled to his party "GET DOWN!"

A swarm of bullets washed over the top of the heads as they semi buried themselves in the loose snow.

"Sie sind auf diese Weise!" a voice rung out.

Terre signalled to the others to scatter by pawing this way and that. The other marked took a few people each and crawled away.

"What did they say?" Rose asked Terre.

"They called out to their friends that 'we are this way'... Let's hope the others aren't having this much grief." His teeth shone in the moonlight.

Together they moved as one, slowly and quietly.

Terre froze. He sniffed the air and he started to flex his claws in and out. Rose needed no explanation as that is when the howling began.

Low, deep and painful to hear. The howl seemed more like a cry, as though someone was being pulled through a mincer legs first.

The air was filled with the sound of heavy panting.

"How is this possible? I thought they could only transform of full moon!?" Terre had transformed back to his human form. He fumbled with a rucksack.

"Maybe they found that thing… the hat of Morgana?" Rose asked questioningly.

"No…" Terre's voice so unsure that even Rose felt a different kind of fear. The one that is felt, when all is lost. "Can't be… Grandfather said…"

He was cut short when out of the fir tree branches launched a large black werewolf. It stood there rocking on its haunches as though it was unsure of its own body. Wrapped around its arm, a red band with the swastika in a white circle.

Terre had dropped the rucksack and had launched fully into the chest of the Werewolf. Green splattered blood sprayed the white snow under it and lumps of flesh and fur scattered to the bark.

Rose watched in fascination. The blood although a strange red to begin with, turned acid green on contact with the silver nails and teeth of Terre's.

Terre had not noticed the three others stumbling from the branches of the treeline. Two ran at Terre whilst his muzzle was down. The other however; had noticed Rose was on her own. Its eyes stared at Rose, confident and cruel.

Rose stood but felt strangely affixed by the stare of the creature.

It lunged and pulled back, as though

teasing Rose with the thought of its vial intentions.

Rose gasped; Terre looked up just in time to notice that he was being stalked.

The first werewolf lunged at Terre but resigned to back off as Terre swiped its face with his claws.

The werewolf that was teasing Rose transformed back to its human form.

"You are a pretty one... for a Zigeuner!"

His voice calm and contemplating.

Terre and Rose found themselves back to back. His fur raised along the ridge of his back.

"It's about now Cousin that we could really do with some natural intervention..." Terre commented.

"I'm not sure that's how..." Rose began to say.

An arrow flew through the air and embedded itself in the back of the taunting Germans head. The arrow head shone silver in the moonlight as the body fell forward and buried itself in the snow

The other two werewolves began to pace looking this way and that.

Terre took his chance and lunged for the jugular that was on show.

Rose turned just in time seeing the

second werewolf lunge for Terre's unprotected flank. She waved her hand and her eyes glowed, feeling the force of the Leyline nearby. It enveloped her in dark thoughts. The nearest branch shot across the opening and buried itself within the guts of the wolf.

Rose felt strange but happy. She turned her gaze on the wolf that fought back against Terre. Vines reached up and grabbed the wolf. Dragging its paws to the ground, whilst Terre ripped around the wolf leaving fresh lesions all over.

Something was wrong. Rose felt a strange sense of longing to not only kill the werewolf but also Terre himself. Before she knew it Terre had also been enveloped by the strangling holds of the vines.

"Cousin... what are... you doing?" the breath was leaving Terre as he struggled against the binds.

A hand grasped firm and strong on Rose's arm. The pain shot through and she lost the train of thought of killing the both of them.

Pasquaile looked at Rose in sympathy.

"I am sorry I am late." His face grave.

"I... erm... "Rose felt as though she were waking from a dream.

Pasquaile went to open his mouth.

A group of trees seemed to explode

from the centre. The wood shattered like glass. Earth rained down as though coming from the sky, stones bit like glass. The explosion forced them all to the snow underneath them.

Rose and Terre stood up again however Pasquaile remained on the ground.

Arrows flew overhead. The sound of twanging of metal against metal and from the treeline, came the form of a gigantic armoured vehicle.

Its turret moved toward the direction of the Fayre who had just loosed their arrows.

The barrel seemed to jerk, as once

again it fired a deathly shell.

The fayre that had not disappeared into the nearest pool of water seemed to come apart at the seams. Arms still holding there bow's clattered into the snow. Boots remained where they stood however that seemed to be the only thing was left.

"RUN!" Terre screamed at Rose.

This time however, Rose was not struck by fear. A deeper anger seemed to come from within her. She yelled from the top of her lungs and pine tree shot up from underneath the tanks body tearing apart the metal and anyone in its way.

Rose's hair came alive as she lifted her

hands up. Her eyes turned from green to purple.

She looked to Terre. "GO!"

Terre went to argue and noticed that somehow Rose had kept control over the pull of the infected Leyline.

More troops and tanks were coming.

A roar in the distance told Terre that the others were in trouble as well.

"Go... Cousin. Save your love!" Rose's voice although struggling with an internal battle, pleaded with him.

He nodded to her and ran.

Rose looked down to the crumpled figure of Pasquaile. Her face darkening even by the moonlight. Her eyes changed to blood red.

Screams in the night came from those who pursued the marked.

Life, Death and Choices

As the sun rose over the horizon, it was met with the strangest of scene's. The usual white snow, now a tapestry of colours. Red's to greens, brown and grey.

Where Rose had stood there now bore a great Oak tree.

The soldier's scavenged around looking for survivors and trophies of their victory of the enemy. They paid no attention to this strange tree even though it stood amongst the bloodiest scene they had ever seen.

Within the tree light glowed from

luminous plants. Rose and Pasquaile covered in moss.

Gradually Rose awakened to her strange surroundings.

"They have dared to poison me..."

"My love, we said we would not interfere with the humans..."

"You interfered... you wrapped this one within yourself to protect. Why can I not use mine to inflict on those who are affecting me?"

"Because we promised not too..."

Rose opened her eyes. "Hello?"

"Oh daughter we are glad you are awake..."

"Am I? Dead?" Rose asked the bizarre voices.

"You are safe now daughter, you alerted us to the poisoning of us..."

Pasquaile began to groan.

"Daughter, there is little you can do for him here..."

Rose felt water rising up around her body.

"Here you will be safe for a time... but do not forget we will need you back!"

A strange rushing sound as though sinking and swimming to the surface at the same time.

Rose opened her eyes. To her disbelief

she laid next to Pasquaile upon a pool within the Grove of the Fayre.

Voices echoed strangely around the wooded glade. Hands soft and firm wrestled them both up and carried them to wooden cots beyond the silken curtains.

*

"She protected him... I saw it mother."

"That as it may it does not answer how she opened a portal to the Grove!"

Rose opened her eyes; moss still

covered her like a thick blanket. She raised her hands to her face and lifted the living vegetation gently off. Light although not glaring still stung her eyes.

"Ah... Good, you are awake Rose." Danu's voice seemed harsh. "Perhaps you can explain how you come to be here with my eldest son, who is still unable to open his eyes..."

Her eyes seem to burn holes through Rose.

"I don't know..." Rose looked at Day through squinted eyes.

Danu huffed and walked out.

"Well you certainly have something

about you Rose Wolbear. I've never seen mother that angry since Morgana travelled to this land by trapping our baby brother." The Fayre woman smiled at her.

Rose sat up and looked about the clearing. On the far cot lay Pasquaile, or rather the moss covered version of him.

"How long have we been like this?" asked Rose.

"About three leaves unfolding..." replied the woman.

Rose looked at her; a quizzical expression lightened her face, the woman just laughed.

"Oh bless you Rose. Your time and our time do not run exactly as you would understand" said the woman.

She tenderly walked over to Pasquaile. "Perhaps you could see if you can wake my brother… "She turned and walked from the room.

Rose looked down upon the moss covered body. When she had properly seen him before he had introduced him to this land. Now however she had managed to somehow travel to this place without his help. She thought about the strange voices that spoke whilst she was within the tree. 'It couldn't be could it? The old religions deities? '

She bent down over Pasquaile and

gently lifted the moss from his face.

His handsome beautifully, sculpted face reminded her of the stone busts of old.

She brushed her hand down his cheek; feeling for imperfections. There were none.

Rose placed her hand on his forehead and a hand upon where his heart was. She leant back, and started to sing.

"*ques ar hé, quasar hé ò..*"a voice in her head spoke. *"Keep going daughter, you have been blessed with all that we can bequeath you. Follow your heart!"*

When Rose finished singing she looked

down. Pasquaile's eyes fluttered open. Rose became locked in his gaze. Inside her head she heard him.

You have called me back... his voice seemed distant. His face portrayed a person weak and vulnerable.

Something about him made Rose forget about where she was or who he was. She leant forward and placed a kiss on his perfect lips. The lips locked, tender and gentle. She opened her eyes and looked at him. His eyes had also closed. She knew this was no Fayrie trap that she had warned about, this was something new and exciting. Her heart raced ahead of her.

A cough in the background made the both of them jump.

"I see my Brother is awake at last. Thank you Rose!" she smiled from the silken wall.

"I... I was just..." Rose stumbled over her words, whereas Pasquaile sat back with a huge smile on his lips.

"Oh you don't need to say anything." She walked back out.

Rose turned back to Pasquaile. Her eyes softened as did his. Something jumped in her mind and panic flushed through her. She had forgotten about her kin.

"I have to get back..." Rose went to leave Pasquaile's side but he held her firm.

Pain shot up Rose's leg above her knee and then along her spine. She almost fell if it were not for the hold Pasquaile had on her.

"You must rest as well... Rose" His voice lifted as he spoke her name.

She steadied herself on the cot of which he lay. Pasquaile sat up and pulled a bowl to his side laden with water.

"You wish to see your kin... here... look" He waived his hand over the surface and before it sat the woods of which only the other night they had left. However this time she saw the soldiers that were coming towards the tree of which they were hidden. Nothing was moving.

The water changed direction and image flitted and honed in on Terre and Gertrude. They were beside the body of Asha. Blood stained all about the snow of which he laid.

"I don't understand why are they not moving?" Rose turned her head and looked to Pasquaile.

"My sister did try and explain to you... time is different here. We are either too fast for your normal time. A year may go by here and yet for you in your time a minute will have passed!"

"Yes and no. The only person who defines the time between our worlds is my mother. She has slowed it so she can analyse what is happening..."

Rose swooned and as she did so
Pasquaile pulled her onto the cot
beside him and together they passed
back into the healing oblivion.

*

Often Rose looked at the bowl to see
the movement of time, but each time
there seemed to be no change from
the last time she had looked.

Her affections with Pasquaile had been
returned by him and they spent hours
upon hours within each other's arms.
He showed her the different delights
of the Grove. The sweets of which

they ate and the purest nectar for which they drank.

The two of them had fallen in love.

Under the light of the pool of years they finally laid together, both with their free will intact.

*

Rose was the first human to have carried a Fayre child without her loss of mind.

A baby boy blessed them some nine months later. His name, Pascal.

"Rose…" Danu's commanding voice echoed through the tree's as Pasquaile, Rose and young Pascal sat together around the pool.

Pasquaile nodded to his beloved and she passed him their baby. Rose gave them both a tender kiss before stepping through the veil towards Danu's hall.

She stared up at the tapestries on the wall. Each one seemed to move and change in it pictures.

"They are the future that may come to pass!" Danu, unknown to Rose had walked to her side. "Every eventuality is not shown but the most probable… are!"

Rose sore people in chambers, naked. Struggling with the throats. Dropping to the floor and men in masks walking in. Another showed men in uniform running for the sea as a thousand black dots flew in their direction.

"This is by far the worst humans have done to each other in their thirst for power." Danu's voice trailed away as she took Rose's hand and walked her away from the devastating scenes that had encaptured Rose with its violence and destruction.

A second chair had formed next to Danu's usual resting place.

Rose didn't resist when she was lead to sit with Danu for she knew that no-one was usually granted permission to sit in her presence.

A click of fingers and strange looking Fayre stepped forward and presented two glasses.

Rose looked into the eyes of the servant and noticed that there was nothing there.

"It is a shame is it not..." Danu spoke so softly it seemed to echo off the walls.

"Why?..." Rose began.

Danu shooed the Fayre away. "Because their parents were tricked into union... You my sons..." Danu chuckled at the thought "lover; has done something that no other has done before. Produced me a grandson with free will!"

Rose looked pityingly at the girl who had just served them...

Danu looked at the concern in Rose's face and attempted to ease her worry. "They are provided for..."

"Yes, but surely..."

"No there is nothing I can do. If I send them back through barrier they will change." she scoffed. "Believe me I tried!"

Danu took a long swig of her drink and turned to Rose.

"I think however we have found a compromise?" Danu's eyes looked

Rose up and down.

Rose felt like a prize bearing heifer. "No... I mean... my family I have to..."

Danu placed a hand on her knee and looked at her, a smile lighting her lips. "I don't mean that you stay here and re-populate my family. I am not and cannot make you stay or do anything you change your will. However I have come to a pass..."

Rose stopped and looked at her.

"I believe that you and your children, even your children's children may bare my children there next generation and giving me my granddaughter and grandsons." Danu stated.

Rose's mind raced over what Danu had just said. "Are you asking me to ask my children to... what carry your children's children?"

"You are a perceptive flower aren't you?" Danu smiled at her.

For some reason it sent a shiver up Rose's spine. She stood because of it.

"No that's..." Rose stumbled at the thought of agreeing to slaving her own children, to the Fayre race.

"Aren't you going to ask what you get in return?" Danu's voice was so smooth it almost caught Rose off guard.

"What... erm... I mean no that's

preposterous..."

"What if I offered safe haven to your clans for whenever and however long they needed, and without any tricks. Letting them leave whenever they liked?" Danu's voice although attempting to stay silken was straining.

Danu clicked her slender fingers and once more two of the will-less Fayre walked forward but this time they held a mirror of moving water. They stopped in front of them.

"You have not been watching over your clan whilst you have been away. Not as much as you did when you first arrived!" Her voice seemed triumphant in tone.

The water swirled and the images of a line of people being pushed along by men in uniform. Clearer the image got and Rose began to see her cousin Terre. Bloody welts down his broken-spirited face. In front was his beloved Gertrude, laced up with binds of woven rope to prevent her moving her hands the rope went about her neck as a noose. Erin was there too trussed much the same with Boet following behind.

"You cannot show me this and do nothing" whimpered Rose. Her heart wishing dearly to rescue her family and friends from the plight they now found themselves in.

"Agree to my terms and we will save them, my word to you as Matriarch!"

Danu placed her hand on Rose's.

Rose closed her eyes. No one in the room heard the next conversation as it were done between Danu and Rose in the voices of their mind.

I agree to your terms, however my kin if they wish, may receive the forgetting for what I have sold them into.

That is understandable Rose. You are wiser than I expected. Very well our deal is DONE.

At the wave of Danu's hand the water enveloped Rose and before she knew it she was spinning right way up close to her captured family.

The cold up on Rose like slipping into an icy stream. She had forgotten how cold it was. In the Fayrie year she had been away.

She looked about her and saw moss covering the nearby log. She leant forward and almost like a cat, it nuzzled into her hand and then spread over her until she became one with the green living fur.

She looked back into the water and there she saw Pasquaile and her son staring after her. Quietly she whispered. "I am sorry my love. I must."

Strong in heart and mind she pulled two hands of freezing water from the stream and strode after the procession.

"Keep the noise down, yer bloody mangy cat!" the man who walked with SS Captain noticed Terre trying to whisper to Boet. He raised a long horse whip and cracked it over his shoulder. "Don't forget, yee can still be shot as a stray!"

A guffaw of laughter followed the comment.

The line was approaching dying Rose bush that had been a rally point for the clans. Terre stared at it intently, wishing for her cousin to return but feeling that it couldn't be.

It was as he passed that a petal fell away. Then another and although no one had noticed new buds were pushing their way out.

Erin fell just before the bush. She landed unceremoniously into the snow.

A rough hand grabbed her by the shoulder.

"Not your time to die yet Witch... but I do believe we have someone who is gonna enjoy taking that gift from you!" The vile stench of rotten meat still came from his jaws.

As Erin came up she saw the red buds flower.

Erin screamed as loud as she could! "GET DOWN!" She kicked the man in the shin and he dropped her back to the not so soft blanket of frozen snow.

Water rained down upon the soldier and the SS Captain. From there followed the screams of those hit as the water took that part of them deep into the Grove.

The man looked this way and that for the one responsible. He could make sense until out of the tree line walked what looked like a moss covered tree.

Rose stared at the man. Anger rose up inside her. The poisoned Leyline no longer affecting her. This time it was all her choosing. She walked among the bodies of the fallen soldiers, almost brushing thin air for where they lay. As she passed they were pulled deeper into the earth.

The man suddenly attacked by the rose bush found himself struggling to free himself from its binds.

She looked him in the eyes. "What's wrong? You look like you have seen a ghost." her eyes narrowed.

"Yer fecking witch. I'm gonna rip your heart out with me bare teeth!" He pushed a hand to his neck and grasped what looked like a pendant. His body convulsing and twisting. Flesh tore open revealing fur.

"Not today you don't!" Terre had recovered and nimbly walked up beside the transforming creature. His paw swung so hard round that the mid transformation head fell from its shoulders, followed by the pendant.

Fenrir, Loki and Hel

The pendant taken from the transforming wolf appeared to be made from a silvery metal.

Terre turned it over and over in his hand whilst they sat by the fire in the woods.

Gertrude and Erin sat side by side watching Rose with a wary look.

"How did you do that thing with the water Rose? I am confused!" asked Boet.

Rose smiled at him. She knew that they would not understand that she had just spent the best part of a year

within the Grove of the Fayre let alone
to have borne a child with them and
laid down a bargain of which, she
could not believe she had agreed to.

"I had a bottle of liquid from the
Fayre. They said I should use it to
ensure victory..."

The answer seemed to settle all those
present, except for Terre. Somehow
he seemed to sense something was
different.

"You cousin seem more... what's the
word?"

Boet in his tactful way spoke over him.
"What your cousin is asking. Why have
you made the moss bigger around
your breasts?"

Rose blushed and then smirked in his direction. "Well a girl has got to have her secrets!"

Terre aimed a clout to the back of Boet's head. "That's the clan leaders Granddaughter and my cousin. Show some respect!" Terre laughed.

"Here let me see that." Erin reached over and grabbed the pendant that was hanging from Terre's hand.

She held it up to the firelight and whispered.

"The gods of my land."

"What was that?" asked Gertrude.

"These symbols on this pendant. They refer to the... let's see, god of mischief. That'll be Loki. Then there is Fenrir the dog that bit its master's hand. Lastly is Fenrir's mother. Hel!"

"That sounds ominous... what does it mean?" Gertrude now stared at the pendant, over Erin's shoulder.

Terre was the one to answer. "It means they now have the ability to change whenever they like!"

It sent them all around the fire silent for a few moments.

"But this thing." Boet pointed to the pendant. "It's got to be made by one who has magic!"

Rose realised what he was saying. "Are you saying that someone with magic has been making these things so that the werewolves can change? If so isn't that against the very nature of the original curse?"

Boet nodded. "Of course. I heard of this kind of magic polluting a Leyline once..."

Everything slotted into place as he said it.

"I know where they are making these!" said Rose.

They all went silent.

A scraping and creaking reverberated from the oak tree from whence Rose and Pasquaile had been cocooned.

Gertrude shook her hands free of Erin

and Terre transformed, sniffing the air for a hint of danger.

Rose stood and walked to the tree. She embraced it as one would do with a loved one. Quietly she whispered to it. The crown of the tree began to twist and turn, it looked like it had grabbed a large bird from the air and like a Venus fly trap grabbed and eaten it alive. A body wrapped in leather fell to the floor.

All five of them now stood over the strange fallen figure.

Murmurs of German came within the folds of the leather.

"Who are you?" said Boet.

Gradually the leather seemed to lift off the body all by itself. It was then that they realised that it wasn't a material as such, but a wing.

The woman under the leather wing looked bedraggled as though she had not slept rough before.

"Eenglish? Ya?" said the woman.

Erin, Gertrude and Rose's eyes instantly turned green. The forest around them seemed to be coming to life.

"Yes we are English. What are you?" Terre spoke in his purring voice.

"Sanctuary!" the woman let out the word as though in desperation.

Terre and Boet helped the woman to her feet, careful and wary to the stranger.

Rose looked her up and down. Something seemed strange about her.

The boys rested the woman close to the fire. She resisted getting any closer as though she were afraid of the leaping flame.

"I saw you…" She pointed to Rose. "You saved that… thing."

Rose looked between Terre and the others. "You mean Pasquaile? The Fayre!"

"I know not what he called; only he smelled strange. Not man… I'm sorry my Eenglish is not good." the woman seemed to be opening up to them.

Terre leaned into her and started to speak in German.

That is when Rose noticed her eyes.

"Terre. Step back!" Rose's voice turned cold.

Terre looked to Rose as though astonished, how could she be afraid; of this frail woman.

"Why are your eyes black as the night sky?" Rose demanded.

"My eyes are this way..." the woman stood up, her body and wings unfolding "because I am not one of you. I am in the old tongue. A nocturne!" She opened her mouth and within shone the teeth like daggers.

A blade came round her throat quicker than lightning.

"Think twice Fallen. We do not interfere but you touch this woman I will break that rule..."

Pasquaile stood behind the woman, ready to slit her throat.

She sagged in his arms.

Rose looked to Pasquaile mentally passing conversation so the others could not hear.

Pasquaile dropped her down to her knees. The others all let out a sigh of relief.

"I have no one to turn too!" she muttered to herself.

Gertrude looked pityingly at the woman. "Tell us, everything!"

The woman revealed that her name was Patricia and that she was born in 1876 on the streets of Dusseldorf. It wasn't until her 40th birthday had this curse been laid upon her.

She retold a story so fantastical that at first it seemed impossible. Trapped by a Count and Countess. Used for her body and treated little more than a slave until she escaped recently to the small village of Zwiesel. The innkeeper, a kind and gentle man told her of the group of Gypsies travelling towards the border, and that they were her safest option of flight.

But then when she had arrived, she saw the snow covered crimson by the Nazi Dogs. Her hope of salvation shrinking.

That was until she saw Rose. Hair flying without wind, protecting a non-human whilst slaughtering and destroying.

The tree came from nowhere and grabbed her about the waste, and then the arms. It pulled her in as though to eat her, but instead it wrapped her against the oncoming rays of the sun.

*

The sun began to rise once more on them, Rose, Gertrude and Erin. Covered Patricia with vines and branches, until the sunlight could not penetrate.

Boet and Erin volunteered to stay near her whilst the others ventured out.

Rose and Pasquaile walked along in virtual silence. Terre had transformed and was running ahead with Gertrude riding his back like a horse.

Gradually the hill became steeper. Forcing them to walk around the gradient rather than straight up.

Smoke appeared in the distance, near to the summit.

"The Leyline. It is close to that smoke." Called Rose to the others.

It took them the best part of the day to walk up the incline but as they got close to the top the view was breath-taking. A stone cairn seemed awkwardly placed as though it had been moved.

Pasquaile looked to Rose. "Can you hear it? The earth is crying!"

Beneath them men beat molten metal with vehemence. A man walked about covered in black drawings.

Rose felt giddy as the proximity to the Leyline started to fill her with its poisoned energy. She looked to Gertrude and noticed that she too was being affected.

Pasquaile slapped Rose round the face to bring her back.

"Thanks, I think" as she nurtured her jaw. She shook her head and then slapped Gertrude to do the same.

Gertrude however became glazed again soon after the slap.

"It's no good. She won't be able to come down with us." said Rose.

Terre looked at Rose with disbelief. "I'm not leaving her again!"

Rose looked between Terre and then to Pasquaile. "This isn't just about you anymore Terre." Her face had changed to a stern look. "We all must sacrifice!"

Pasquaile placed a hand on Rose's shoulder. "I will take her to the Grove. She will recover there!"

Rose nodded to Pasquaile, bringing fresh complaints from Terre. "No..." he began.

It was too late. Pasquaile and Gertrude vanished off the peak.

*

Night fell and in the distance gigantic wings flapped through the air carrying two large objects.

Patricia landed with Boet and Erin held firmly to her breast.

Boet walked shakily over to Terre. "I think I am in love brother. That woman could take me to heaven and back." He cheekily winked at Terre and then walked over and gave Rose a hug.

"How are you feeling Patricia?" Rose asked.

She looked about her. "There is many wolves nearby. Are you sure this must be done?"

"I'm afraid it must!" Rose spoke in earnest of the task ahead.

Terre and Boet changed into their cat form and slipped away toward the entrance to the caves. Erin and Rose walked together watching the events unfold.

Terre and Boet jumped the guards from behind forcing them to roll down the hill. A third guard came running out, before he could shout a hand shot out from the darkness of the sky above and lifted him fully into the night sky.

The body dropped some leagues away. Drained off his life blood.

Rose and Erin crept forward toward the tunnel entrance. A train sat slowly puffing smoke. Men hauled small metal medallions to a hopper and then loaded the hopper straight into the train.

"You are sure that this will give

everything you have promised Herr Sven?"

"And more Herr Captain. Zey will give your troops who are infected the gift of change whenever they wish and with it the impenetrable gift of ze lycan." It was the man with the drawings on his skin.

"Vot part of our beloved country have they promised you mage!" a voice shouted from the hopper.

The man did not appear German.

The mage lifted a finger and the man's chain about his neck tightened so much that he began to choke.

"You dare address me! I will come for

your family with the Wolf Wache and then let you watch!" the mage laughed at the thought of it and then released the man into a fit of choking and crying.

In a whisper. "We have to set these men free!" said Erin.

"Yes but how?"

"Up there the timbers that hold this place aloft. We could bring this place down?!" she said it in such a way that Rose knew the poisoned Leyline was beginning to affect her.

"Leyline first!" Rose brought a hand round quickly and slapped Erin in the face. "I need you. I can't do this alone and neither can you!"

Both Rose and Erin skirted round the train out of site of the men working a way.

They stopped near the back of the last carriage to see the Mage walk past. His skin was full of symbols to the Norse gods. His beard and hair long and platted, served as a covering for his torso.

The girls watched him walk away from the main cavern, and decided to follow him.

A large tunnel, lead away from the main processing area. The hammers that fell; gradually fell silent as they walked.

It was eerie how silent it was.

From the distance a cry of pain echoed out. The ripping of material and the eager laughter that followed made the girls wish for the eerie silence once more.

Flame light flickered on the cavern that now was in front of them. The mage, on his knees in front of altar, behind that altar stood the largest wolf she had ever seen. Its spittle spraying red as a piece of cloth dangled in its jaws.

Another voice rang out. "Where are these others you promised us?!"

A gaunt woman stood looking into a naked green light.

"I cannot poison Yggdrasil without

more blood of the gifted." He picked up the mage as though he were a feather. "Maybe I should use yours next..."

"My lord Loki.... I..."

"I am trapped, unless Ragnorak happens soon we will be noticed and I... I will have to go back!"

The woman turned around. Her face a mixture of beauty and horror. "You have only thought of yourself... that is why we have not succeeded." She grabbed the mage from the clutches of Loki. "And you. We have given you the blessing you wanted, now fetch me more blood!"

The mage stumbled about clutching at

his throat. He had not noticed the girls hidden behind the rock.

"So what now?" Erin looked completely amazed.

Rose looked at her in disbelief. "We are here to stop them. Aren't we?"

"Do you realise who they are... they're the gods of my land... well ok the evil ones but..." She was stumbling over her words.

"Erin. I'm sorry but I am not caring if these are Gods, Nazi's or what. I have sacrificed too much to be here to save our clans.... So think. What can we do?"

Erin went quiet and started fiddling

with her chain. Behind her St Christopher another pendant hung. Mjolnir.

Erin's fingers wrapped around it and she fell into a silent prayer.

Rose grabbed her hand. "This is Thor's hammer, correct?"

"Yes, but..." Answered a bewildered Erin.

"I have an idea!" Rose smiled, it was a maniacal smile.

She pulled Erin to her feet. Clasping the hand tight.

"Oi..." Shouted Rose.

Fenrir growled deeply, Hel and Loki

turned and scorned there approach.

"Look Loki. Blood freely given!" Hel's voice cold and malicious.

Loki pulled a scythe free from a body that lay nearby.

"Wonders will never cease...!"

Rose pulled Erin closer. "Look up!"

As Erin looked high to the cavern ceiling she noticed the growing vines weaving in and out of the surface.

Erin looked back at Rose. "You're not thinking."

Rose raised her hands, whilst still clasping onto Erin's.

"I understand why you hide! Shame though. I rather like fresh air!" Rose's hands dropped. As she did so the ceiling of the cavern did the same.

"Stupid girl! You think that can stop us?" Loki mocked. Brushing the earth from his shoulders.

"No." Rose held the Erin's hand that still held the symbol of Mjolnir. She raised it high above their heads. "But he can!"

The sky once clear above, now swirled with darkened clouds. Light flashed around it in a turbulent festoon of colour.

Lightening rained down upon the three gods of old. It seemed that only moments passed. But when the light cleared, Hel, Fenrir and Loki had gone.

"Who are you?" The mage was running back up the passage. He was pulling a large black knife from his belt.

Rose looked to Erin.

"I will die happy now. I know the sky gods still look after us!" said Erin.

"You ain't finished yet, girl." Rose smirked.

She raised both of their hands and together they sent the vines like serpents running through the caverns ceilings.

"I'm glad to have met you Rose!" Erin

smiled back at her.

With an almighty pull with all there will. The caverns ceilings erupted. Stone and earth moved downwards with a deafening crash. The mage seeing what they were doing; ran to escape the falling debris.

Just as he reached them, a large boulder struck him between the blades of his shoulder. His mouth opening and closing as though trying to gain breath.

After the dust settled; the two girls stood holding each other. Tears filled their eyes. But this time it was in joy.

The Nazi's would not get there unstoppable army, as each one of the pendants had been buried and crushed along with the mage who had made them.

"So... any ideas how to get out?" Asked Erin.

Sanctuary

Both Erin and Rose had been lifted from the cavern by their new ally, Patricia. She had flown them to the inn keeper in the heart of Zwiesel. Within the basement's basement they rested up. Trying to make sense of the events that had taken place during the last few days.

For Rose it was harder. For her she had just spent well over a year within the Grove and yet for everyone else time had stood still.

Rose sat in the darkened cellar thinking of her child. Never being able to look upon him each day.

Patricia was the only one that seemed to notice.

"You are sad?" Patricia approached the crouched figure of Rose.

"I merely wish to be out in the air" Lied Rose.

Patricia chuckled. "I have heard this lie before. It is not my business."

Rose looked up at her. She was beautiful for an older lady. With this thought, she smiled. "Men must have paid dearly to spend a night with you!"

Patricia sat beside her. "Yes, they did. But I also paid an awful price. I never had anyone to care for me, nor to love me..." Her head hung low.

"You said there are others like you. Can you not find another to share with?" Rose enquired.

"The others like me. Well, I guess there hearts are dark from the wanting of the blood lust. I don't know if I find anyone who teeters like I, on the edge of darkness and light!" Patricia's words haunting and lonely.

"I tell you what... you survive this war and I'll promise you that I'll find others for you to spend your years with... just like a mother hen!" Rose smiled.

"I would like that! Who knows I might even open a bar..." Patricia began to smile.

"You could call it the Dancing Devil!"

Rose smiled back at her.

"Yes I like that!"

*

The collapse and explosions at the Wolf Wache base reverberated through the Third Reich so much so that the SS came down hard on all the residents surrounding Zwiesel.

The remaining villagers were too scared to hide the Gypsies and there strange friend.

Eventually they knew they had to leave Germany.

Terre and Gertrude travelled south to the borders of Switzerland. Boet and Erin ventured west. Leaving only Rose and Patricia to travel north.

The roads swarmed with military trucks and vehicles. From above the towns looked like an ants nest. Constant lines of dark figures traveling to and from.

Germany had begun its further invasion of Europe.

By late 1940 Patricia and Rose had become the talk of legend in varying resistance movements. The two women who had battled their way across the land. Leaving a bloody destruction behind them and so far the SS had not found a way to defeat them.

Rose and Patricia had made their way

to Dusseldorf. Patricia's hometown.

She wept as she walked the cold streets. Looking at various buildings and remembering.

"This is where my mother died…" She said to Rose as they walked the cooling streets.

Rose placed a hand, in her's. "You are not alone anymore." She squeezed her hand to remind her of that.

A church loomed out from the darkness.

"Do you mind if we visit the mausoleum? My mother is buried there!"

Rose did not need to answer.

The great doors creaked open.

"Zis is the house of God!" those were the first words from the Priest that out from the cloisters.

"I'm sorry Father. I have travelled a great many miles to visit my mother's grave!"

The priest held up his lantern. It lit their faces and the priest dropped it at the sight of them. Thankfully Patricia caught it and Rose caught the falling Priest.

They traded what they had caught and Patricia carried the priest to the altar.

Rose looked at the priest's hand.

There upon was the mark of the order of Ezekiel.

Patricia stalked off to the tombs, leaving Rose above.

"Father... wake up!" She splashed little droplets of water in his face.

"Wos ist zis." he began.

"I'm sorry father but my Deutch is still somewhat basic." She pulled up his hand and traced the symbol on his hand. "You are a member of the order!"

The priest shook his head.

"Who are...?"

"I am Rose, Father."

"Danke Rose... vere ist..?"

"Lie still father."

The priest sat bolt upright. "Is not right. She cannot be here!" He almost fell over getting off the podium for which he had been laid.

He hurried down to the large double doors. It took all of his effort just to swing one of the heavy doors enough for him to go through.

Rose marched after him. She did not fear for Patricia, more the other way.

They found Patricia kneeling in front of a wall stone.

It read to my departed mother. 'May God accept you into his arms.'

Patricia wept uncontrollably.

The priest almost skidded to a halt. His hands crossed his body so many times Rose felt that he was going to take off.

Rose barged past him and placed a hand on her shoulder.

"You can't be here!" the priest began mutter. He faltered as he looked at the date and name of the deceased.

"Shut... Up!" Rose's eyes illuminated in t candlelight.

Patricia stayed on her knees for some time; Rose knelt beside her.

The priest realising that he wasn't going to move them walked back to the cloisters.

*

By Morning Rose kissed Patricia on the head and went off to the priest.

He busied himself in the small kitchen; a small transistor radio sat playing propaganda speeches...

A name came up on the radio that she recognised. WINSTON CHURCHILL.

"Father, what was that about Winston?"

The priest practically threw his breakfast all over the stove.

"Could you knock next time Froiline?"

He looked at the mess, picked up his rosary, said a silent prayer and then started cleaning up.

"I'm sorry father. I have spent long in the shadows that I forget my manners."

"I do understand my child... Are you the same as her?" he looked at her with a piercing gaze.

"Oh... no father I am Wolbear. Rose Wolbear."

His eyes widened. "You are are her? Your Gross Father, he has been looking for word of you..." the priest shuffled over to stone depiction of the cross. He pushed it and twisted it and a panel slid across to the side. It revealed a crude radio with a button. As he turned it on small bleeps came through from the speakers.

The post pulled up a stool and sat down, twisting and turning the knobs in a furious manner. He pulled a lever and it seemed to let out a strange tone.

After a minute the bleeps in the background ceased. He muttered under his breath.

"Urgent news. stop. Wolbear daughter safe stop location docks stop"

The bleeping went silent. After which the radio went crazy with sound.

A bell began to ring just above his

head. Quickly the priest shut off the bleeping machine and slid everything back into its place. He turned and looked at her. "Hide!" his voice was but a whisper.

"Herr Hochwürden!" came a shout from the pews.

The priest hurried out.

Rose swept the whole room with her gaze. Apart from squeezing through the small window by the sink, she didn't have much option.

Voices got louder and more ferocious. The priest voice rasping as though he were being throttled. Then silence.

"Englander, we know you are here!

Come out or we will smoke you out!"

Rose stayed stock still, hoping that they didn't walk in on her.

Numerous boots stomped about outside. Pews were overturned. Metal clanged to the stone floor.

Finally doors slammed.

Rose looked out into the church. The priest lay crumpled on the floor.

She rushed over to him. His forehead bleeding, his eyes glazed but at least he was breathing.

"Father... Can you hear me?" She shook him.

Nothing.

She started pulling him towards the great doors that lead to the mausoleum.

The other end of the church she could see smoke start billowing from the doors.

Panicking she slipped on the floor. A hand caught hold of her mid fall.

A tall man wearing battered clothing had come out of nowhere and now held her.

"I'm sorry Froi-line I don't speak a lot of German, but... I want to help you!" His voice soft and calm.

"You're the one they're after...?" Rose stared, eyes wide as it dawned on her.

They didn't know she was here.

"English eh. Well I won't ask why you're here; let's get this chap downstairs. He's got a way out!" He nodded towards the priest they were dragging.

Rose merely nodded and carried on pulling.

As they got to the under croft the stranger left Rose with the priest and went back to the door. He pushed it closed and pulled a large solid wooden bar across the doors.

"Bloody krauts. Don't worry dear they'll dampen the flames shortly!" He winked at her and then returned to pulling the priest along.

Shouts from above signalled the return of the soldiers.

"Blimey. They really want me." He let out a small chuckle although his eyes looked haunted.

The priest began stir. His voice mumbling in German.

"Come on Michiel, you did well." reassured the man.

The priest merely mumbled back.

A large thumping noise came from the double doors. "EINE, ZWEI, DREI..." Thump and then a creak.

"Oh bloody Nora. That's a first!" The man looked more than scared. He looked petrified.

A shadow passed over the candlelight. He almost jumped out of his skin went Patricia laid a hand on his shoulder.

"Und you are..." She said quietly.

"Just laid an egg..." the man replied.

The creaking changed to a cracking noise; then a shearing.

Patricia looked up over his shoulder. The man shivered as he felt the air move over him.

Patricia flew past the candles, blowing them out as she went.

"Stay down..." Rose whispered.

Flashes of muzzle fire lit the room; screams shouted out in pain. Rose felt the warm splatter of blood cover her. Metal landed next to them.

Patricia dropped the ripped limbs holding the machine guns, from the protesting bodies of the soldiers that hunted them.

Finally a single match lit. A German SS commander stood, holding it. He shook in fear as he looked at the blood soaked glove that held the match box of which he had struck.

A woman's face appeared in front of him. She seemed beautiful to begin with, her lips crimson red. Her smile, alighting the strange looking teeth. Her eyes were pure black.

"Sanctuary?" he whispered.

Puff

The match went out. And a gurgling noise echoed through the tunnels.

Homecoming

With the priest's help Rose, Patricia and the Englishman escaped through the tunnels to a small row boat waiting on the River Rhine. They travelled mostly at night to avoid detection from the patrols.

The Englishman turned out to be a Pilot Officer by the name of Bill Osterbeck from the Royal Air Force. He had escaped from a prisoner of war camp close to Dusseldorf and had been fortunate to have found his way to the church.

*

"A few more miles and we will have reached the borders of Germany." stated the priest. "We will head for my Brothers church. St Peter Canisius in Nijmegen."

"As much as I would like to stay with you Padre and you ladies. I must get back to Bomber Command!" Bill grinned.

Patricia looked at Rose.

"If we survive this..." began Rose.

"I will open my bar. Dancing Devil..." She began to laugh.

Rose pulled Patricia into an embrace. "I owe you such a debt..."

"And I you!" Patricia said.

Tears began to roll down their cheeks.

"If ever you need me, send word and I will come!" Patricia whispered.

Rose turned to Bill. "I too, must get back to my family." Rose thought of Terre, Erin, Boet and Gertrude. Wondering if they had made it back yet.

"It looks to me Padre like I'm getting the fairer of the deals here." Bill smirked.

The priest however smiled and placed his hand into Patricia's. "If it is one thing that God has taught me. Is that Angel's; come in many forms!"

*

Patricia and Priest parted there way at the close to the centrum of Nijmegen.

Bill and Rose carried on sailing down the River Waal.

*

Following the rivers flow to the east, Rose and Bill; one evening, saw a lantern swinging to and fro on the water.

"Hado!" Shouted a voice. "Lekker Avond.!"

Bill froze to the spot. A pole still in his hand.

As though in slow motion, a canal boat sidled up to them.

Rose looked around for any kind cover she could hide them in, however there was none.

The boat owner his hand raised higher in the air.

"Engels?"

Rose looked down into the rippling water. To her surprise a face was looking back. It winked at her and then disappeared. She thought she recognised it.

"It's ok... Mother!" Another voice floated over the water.

Rose was the one to become frozen to the spot.

"It is me.... Pascal."

The barge moored up at a landing jetty.

"This is the BiesBosch mother." The calm words from her son made everything surreal.

"You shouldn't be..." Rose began.

"Father showed me your struggles and although Grandmother did not want me to come she says that I have your will!"

Bill looked between Pascal and Rose. "Certainly look young for your age Rose!" He exclaimed as he looked to the youthful teenager and then back to Rose.

Rose looked at Bill in such a way that

he decided to join the captain of the boat.

Rose pulled Pascal into her. She felt overwhelmed. Her son had grown up without her. He clasped onto her and held her in a comforting embrace.

Finally Rose pulled slightly away and held his head in her hands.

"How so much your father you look! How is he?"

"Worried. He watches you every day. Since you destroyed the poisoning Grandmother agreed to speed up the time again between our lands."

"I have missed you!" Tears began to form at the creases of her eyes again.

"I cannot stay long." The words every mother dreads to hear. "But Father has an idea!"

Pascal took his mother down into the bowels of the barge along with the Dutch man and Bill.

Bill and the Dutchman stood under deck, both holding a glass each of Scotch.

"PROST!" said the Dutchman

"Bottoms up! Chin chin." replied Bill.

Rose looked between them both.

"Don't worry Rose, this chap is resistance. Jolly good luck to have landed us here to be honest!" Bill held out his glass to be filled once more.

Rose turned to her son. "Who is this man?"

Pascal pointed to the man's artwork on the walls. Large Ravens were shown in flight or perched upon the carrion.

How did Rose miss it? She half whispered to herself. "Wolraven"

"Ja that is us." He smiled "I am Marten." from the other end of the barge came a little boy. "This is my son. Werner."

"You Rose..." Werner turned to his father. "Vader ist Rose? Ja?"

"Ja Werner." Marten stroked his head and waved him off.

Instead Werner ran over and gave Rose a huge hug and then ran off in another direction.

Rose looked at Marten. "He has the mark?"

Marten didn't smile back. "He has. It is his mother's gift to him."

The uneasiness in his voice made Rose realise that not everyone wanted their children to grow up and become werewolf hunters.

"Please let's sit." Marten showed them to a bench.

Pascal poured water onto the table top. Bill went to rise but Rose placed a hand on him and bid him to sit.

Pascal's hand passed over the table and the land of the BiesBosch came into focus as though it were daylight. Even the barge could be seen. Gradually it zoomed out.

Bill sat stock still. Rose was sure that looking at his reaction, his limit, was believing Patricia was some sort of magician with wings.

She placed a hand on his thigh. "It's ok..."

Pascal nodded to his mother and then waved once more and the land zoomed away; showing the town of Geertruidenberg and then of Breda. Wider the map grew until it stopped.

It looked like bees swarming in and

out. It took a moment but even Bill started to realise what it was. It was a Luftwaffe Airfield.

Bill placed a hand on hers and leant in.

"This is perfect!"

"Father thinks the same!" said Pascal as he waved it again and showed the Airfield in almost perfect clarity.

"There's a Junker 33. That would be perfect..." Bill seemed over joyed. "But how do we get there?"

Pascal looked to Marten. "We will get you there!"

The image wavered and then dissipated as Pascal held out a flask and seemingly poured the liquid back into it.

"Now it is time for me to go!" said Pascal in a defeated voice.

Rose took her hand from Bills and clasped Pascal's hip. "I will walk you back!"

Rose and Pascal walked back to the barge's, off and around the jetty and then into the reeded waters.

Rose knelt down and touched the water. A light illuminated. In the light shone back the image of her love Pasquaile. "Thank you." she whispered. He winked at her and then his image was gone.

Pascal placed his hand on her shoulder. "We will see each other again mother... I promise!" He alighted a kiss on her head and then he walked forward and the water consumed him until all that was left was a memory in the ripples.

As she stood to walk away and all familiar voice rang out.

"Do not forget our deal!"

Rose nodded almost to herself and then walked back on board.

*

The barge took them through Oosterhout's waterways and along to the banks of Dongen. The barge;

under the cover of dusk, moored briefly to let out two of its passengers. It then continued on its way as though nothing had happened.

The quickest route was across the fields.

Earth stuck to their feet as they slogged through the muddy fields.

Lights shone brightly from the Airfield close by. Voices shouting instructions although inaudible were certainly in German.

"Oh how many times we've bombed this place." Reminisced Bill.

Rose looked at him with the light of the lamps from the field. "What?"

"Gilze Rijen" Bill offered his hand in the direction of the airfield. "Bloody Krauts harass us from here. Either going out or going home!"

Gradually they got closer. Bills gasped seemed to be getting longer, as he spotted a different plane on the runway.

"I can't believe it. Messerschmitt 109's, Junkers 88's... no wonder we've been warned off flying this way." Exclaimed Bill.

"You really are talking Dutch to me..." Rose smile softened something in his heart.

"Before we commit this suicide Rose. I just want to say..."

"Links, Recht. Links, Recht..." a passing squad of German guard marched past.

Rose waited for them to pass. "You're welcome Bill!" She winked and then hopped over the ditch and ran for the fence.

"But... oh sod it. In for a penny..." Bill followed Rose.

As he got to the fence he noticed that the metal wire had been somehow bent out of shape and was twisted in ivy.

"Psst... this way!"

Bill squeezed through the gap and followed Rose ran around the side of a hangar. To her surprise; she ran straight into a soldier leaning on the wall with a cigarette. The cigarette went flying as he pulled his machine gun level with his hip.

"Achtung!" he yelled.

Rose put her hands up in the air just as Bill came round the corner and curled his fist up and rounded it on his chin.

The soldier crumpled to the floor.

"Well that's let the cat out of the bag..." Bill lent down and grabbed the man's machine gun. "Help me drag this into the shadows..."

Boots came stomping down the

runway.

"Too late! Rose run!"

Bill took off in the opposite direction to the feet. Rose took the hint and followed.

They sheltered at the back of another hangar.

Whistles blew out into the night air.

"We've got a cat in hell's chance of getting out of this!" Bill pulled the magazine out to check how many bullets he had, then pushed it back in.

Rose peered round the corner. An aeroplane sat slightly proud of its hangar just a hundred feet away.

"Bill what about that one?"

Bill almost doubled in laughter. "A Junker 33? It's just a transport plane. No weapons!"

"Doesn't matter! Would it get us home?"

"Well of course but the moment we get airborne the Ack Ack is going to blow us out of the sky!"

"Leave that to me!" Rose's voice stern and commanding.

Bill ran with Rose to the Junker.

A German pilot sat on the wing. He saw Rose first and started to unbutton his tunic.

He stopped half way down as Bill stuck the machine gun in his stomach.

"Rouse Kraut! I'm commandeering your kite!" Gingerly the pilot climbed down.

He turned to slip off the wing but as he turned he had picked up a wrench.

Rose kicked the man in his testicles. He bent over; crippled by the blow.

"That wasn't very nice, now was it..." Bill brought the butt of the rifle down on his head.

Bill climbed over his body and climbed into the pilot seat.

Rose followed him in.

"Have you taken the chocks off?" Bill asked.

She looked at him in bewilderment.

"The wheels have blocks, just pull them out and we can get back to Blighty..." as Rose jumped back out he muttered. "Or end up in a ditch again!"

He pulled the nobs and twisted the dials.

Rose jumped back in with rope and wooden blocks dangling in her hand. "Well?"

"Don't need them!"

Rose leaned out and threw the chocks away. Slapping the stunned pilot once more in the privates.

The engine kicked over.

"Come on girl!" Bill whispered to the aeroplane.

On the second fire the blades started turning.

"A-ha!" Bill cried in joy.

The Junker rolled forward onto the airfield. Other planes were starting to taxi out onto the runway.

"Now would be a good time to show me how we're not going to get shot down!"

A rattle of machine gun fire and holes pierced the hull.

"It was nice knowing you!" Bill was almost resigned to the fate.

"Just get this thing in the air!"

Rose opened the window so she could see the attacker. The wind pushed her hair around her. She focused on him and the grass under his feet pulled him to the floor.

More soldiers came out to the screams. The Junker finally on the runway.

The engine revved higher and higher. "Tally-ho!"

It leapt forward with a jolt but strangely Rose stood stock still. In her mind she saw the airfield as Pascal had shown them.

The planes that were in front of them beginning the ascent were strangely dragged back down to earth with explosions as they hit the anti-aircraft guns.

The Junker was finally in the air.

As it climbed Rose felt complete freedom.

*

"115 SQUADRON RAF. THIS IS BOMBER BILL FLYING A STOLEN JU 33. COME IN PLEASE OVER."

"115 SQUADRON RAF. THIS IS BOMBER BILL FLYING A STOLEN JU 33. COME IN PLEASE OVER."

"UNKNOWN PILOT THIS IS 115 SQUADRON. IDENTIFY CHARLIE OVER."

"115 SQUADRON. THIS IS BOMBER BILL. IDENTIFYING CHARLIE. SIERRA NOVEMBER OSCAR ROMEO INDIAN NOVEMBER GOLF OVER."

"BOMBER BILL WELCOME HOME! LAND SOUTH SIDE OF AIRFIELD AND PREPARE FOR HOMECOMING!"

Epilogue

Rose and Bill landed in RAF Little Snoring in 1943.

Bill continued to fly the Lancaster's even after his quota was done, he continued. He said it was because of the people he had seen suffer; deserved his perseverance.

Rose was greeted by Grampy Wolhawk. Her Grandfather had sadly died in a fire after he returned to save the occupants; who were trapped in a house collapse.

She travelled south and busied herself by learning how to mend fighter planes.

Terre and Gertrude arrived back from Switzerland. Terre took over as the head of the Wolbear clan.

Boet and Erin were not heard from again. Although the clan never gave up hope!

Patricia worked hard with the priest and fought against the Germans in Arnhem. In 1945 she returned to the church in Nijmegen and was granted a form of freedom by an Angel who appeared to her, she started her bar 'Dans Duivel'.

Bill and Rose met during the VJ Day celebrations in Essex. They fell in love and had a child. She was named Erin, after the friend she had lost.

Rose chose to marry Bill after they had been together for 10 years and she took his name, Osterbeck.

When Erin came of age, Rose kept her bargain but enacted the right of forgetfulness.

Finally Rose saw a symbol in her leaves as her first fully human Grandson was born.

She never read the leaves again!

Lastly a little note from me the Author...

Well I wanted to say thank you for actually reading this bit... but if you didn't you won't realise this is the end. Yes dear Rose is of course now stuff of legend for Ethan. John the Fallen Angel meets Rose once in his life but then why should I spoil that encounter.

The characters in this story are not linked to any real person, so if I killed someone with your name. Don't feel it's a personal thing...

Dedication of this...

I'd like to dedicate this to my family and friends who put up with me speaking about nothing but my writing adventures.

Special mention

Rose – My Grandmother I wish we had more time together.

Leeann – My Wife for giving me time to finish what I have started.

To my sons – Never give up on a dream. Persevere endure but never give up!

Sarah B, Charlotte M and Adam C – For being my Beta Reader! ☺

Laura from justpublishit.com for an amazing front cover!!

Crystal and Cayce – For helping me with the blurb!! You guys are fantastic!!

Inside info

For hints of what is going to happen in the next story come join me Facebook @StoriesbySIG or Twitter @SIGStories

Other stories:

The Last Shadow Warrior Book 1
The Last Shadow Warrior Book 2

Wolfsbane The Mark Book 1
Fallen Angel Am I (Order of Ezekiel series)

Shorts

Past Memories: Cradle to Grave
Fear, Helplessness and Chains
Spawn of the Net

Poetry

Poetry from a Twisted Bar

Printed in Poland
by Amazon Fulfillment
Poland Sp. z o.o., Wrocław